ANTIDOTE

TAYLOR HONDOS

Taylor Hondos

Antidote

Cover Design by Ashley Ruggirello

Edited by Measha Stone

Previously published as The Antidote, Booklocker.com, 2014

Print ISBN : 978-1-927940-54-9

EPUB ISBN : 978-1-927940-55-6

To my family, who taught me to never give up on my dreams.

Antidote

Part One: Lena

Prologue

I STEPPED INTO the full auditorium. The chatter of the audience was nerve racking, even though I was used to feeling anxious when it came to dancing. It was to be my very last recital; I was going to be done with for good. I knew I would graduate from high school, but I had my mother to thank for graduating from my favorite hobby. I was a dancer from the age of eight, and danced recreationally for half my life. It felt strange to tuck that part of me away for good. My mother always inspired me to continue when I felt I would fail. My dad was great, but he worked so much. He didn't make it to a lot of my performances, which made it even more surprising when I spotted him walking toward me with my mother. He looked a little nervous, but my mother was beaming at me. She moved swiftly toward me, even though I knew it pained her to even stand on her leg.

"Hi, sweetie," she said as she kissed my cheek.

I gave my best smile through the nerves. "Hi, Mom."

"We're so excited. Aren't we?" She nudged my father, and he gave a stiff nod. My mother winced as she switched the weight off her right foot to the left. My heart sank a little.

My mother walked with a horrible limp, which she obtained from the rotting that began from her calf and ran all the way up her thigh.

For exactly one year, the world had lived in fear of the deadly disease Dermadecatis, or by the name most called it "The Black Sickness."

It caused rotting to occur and would spread rapidly throughout the body in a matter of days. The disease was completely lethal, and there was no cure. It began as a small black dot, increasing to the size of a large bruise. Some even mentioned signs of lumpy skin, but most people only got a bruise. The bruise would last a few days, and for those who got the disease, rarely did they realize it before it was too late. Max and his mother lived next door, and his mother lived just six days after the bruise was sighted. He never even looked in anyone's direction anymore. He was afraid that if he gazed too long at anyone, they would fall victim too.

Nobody knew how the disease spread, but my mother was convinced it was airborne. My father was convinced otherwise. He was the lead research doctor of Dermadecatis. My father's name is Dr. Alona or to his colleagues, Sebastian Alona, and he was the first doctor to realize that something odd was happening. Isaac was the first victim of the disease. My dad discovered it in him a month before the full outbreak. After three days of tests and failed treatments, Isaac died. My father worked with many patients since then, but none of them lasted more than two weeks, except for my mother. She was diagnosed with the disease six weeks ago, and if not for my father making remedies to keep the disease at bay, she would probably have died a month ago. The rotting wouldn't leave her leg and it was slowly spreading. Sometimes I feared I would contract the disease from her, but I never did.

My mother was beautiful, and her eyes glistened even now. She looked tired, but she was always glowing and radiating beauty. She had blonde hair and blue eyes, but I did not favor her like I did my father, and in a way, I preferred it that way. He had brown hair and hazel eyes, which I both possessed. He never smiled, except a smug, toothless smile whenever he felt as if it was appropriate.

Sometimes I found myself wondering what day it would be that my mother was going to leave this earth. One day, she was healthy, and the next, she was rotting from the leg down. It spread more each day, and we were afraid of what would happen to her next. My father watched her with wistful eyes, as if he knew how to help her, but couldn't bring himself to do it. I would only have my dad if this got any worse. He was always busy in his office, trying to find the cure for this, and I feared I would be on my own. He and his partner seemed to be having a "break through" as he called it, but I was not so sure.

"Nervous?" Mom asked in her soft tone. She tucked a strand of my hair behind my ear and held her hand on my cheek as if to examine me.

"You'd think I'd be used to this kind of thing, but I'm not prepared for the senior slideshow." Ever since I was a little girl, I wanted to sit among my friends and burst in to tears because we all knew it would never be the same again. After all, how many times do you graduate from dance and high school? My mother smiled and nudged my cheek with her hand in encouragement.

My dad stood awkwardly beside her. His face tightened. He seemed to be anxiously deciding in his brain the appropriate thing to say, but he just stared off into space as he often did now when his thoughts became too much. Ever since my mother got sick, he never seemed to know what he should say or do to make things better. He worked diligently to find a cure. He loved her, and it was apparent. He had a troubled look in his eyes every time he gave her one of his new remedies.

"Dad, are you okay? You look really worried. Did you miss work for me? You can go back. Really, it's okay," I told him. He continued to stare blankly until he finally registered what I had said. I felt embarrassed for disturbing his thoughts, but I didn't want him to be there if he was uncomfortable.

"Everything is fine, Lena." He kissed the top of my head. "I've been saving this for the right time, and this seems like the perfect time for your graduation gift. It's not much, and your real gifts are coming, I promise," he added gingerly with a smile. He held out a white box, and I took it in my hands. I opened it, and inside held a beautiful necklace that held a large, golden key. On top of the key, there were circles enclosing a diamond heart. I looked at him in surprise and felt the grin spreading across my face. "I know it isn't much, but I want you to wear it. One day you might see the true beauty within it. Just like you'll find in yourself one day. You hold the key to your happiness, and this is just a reminder." He held his breath as if he wanted to cry, and I felt my breath catch as well. He cleared his throat and continued. "But enough with this. I miss this stuff a lot, and I want to be here for this. Go get ready and we'll be watching you. We love you." He put the necklace on me in one swift movement, and my heart fluttered. I looked down at it and smiled. He kissed my head again. I stretched around and held him in a tight embrace as my mother clasped her hands together, smiling brightly. We pulled apart, and my father smiled. He held my gaze longer than normal.

"Go, get ready, darling. We love you," my mom said softly. She looked into my eyes. "You mean the world to me, Lena, and always remember that."

My mom blew a kiss to me, and I was oddly panicked as they walked away. My dad didn't seem right. I caught sight of my mom ducking her head as my dad shielded her from my view. But I could still see, and her face was full of terror.

Before I had time to think, I was being rushed to the dressing room. My opening number was first up, and we all had to be ready in five minutes. Thank God I was already dressed and ready for the dance. My hands shook, and it wasn't from nerves anymore. What if this was what my father had warned us about?

My dance team and I walked onto stage and we faced the back wall with our backs to the curtains. My best friend, Kaley, looked over to me. She mouthed quickly, *Are you okay?* and I stiffly nodded. The curtains rolled up, and I put on the fakest smile I could muster as the lights beamed on my back. The music began, and suddenly everything went silent and the auditorium went black as night. There was a wave of movement and panicked shouts. A piercing scream came from the center of the auditorium.

There was uproar, but through the screams, I heard my name being called over and over again. I jumped from the stairs uneasily, and broke into a run toward the voice. It was being carried from the auditorium and into the lobby.

In the lobby, there was nothing but eerie silence. I felt around on the walls with my hands and felt dampness on my feet. Before I could panic, the lights flickered on, and I looked down to see the floor coated in blood. On it, my father stared sightlessly at the ceiling. He was already gone. I felt my heart shatter. I found my mother moving toward me on the floor. I began to sob because I knew she was going to die.

I screamed for help, but no one seemed to hear; they just stared obliquely into the distance, as if to give me time to say goodbye. I didn't want that so I shouted louder at them until I felt a hand on my leg. I kneeled next to my mother. She reached for me, and I took her hand. She shook her head as if to say no, it is too late. She waved me closer and began choking. I was sobbing so hard I could barely hear her.

"Be safe, my Lena." And then she was gone.

I sat there, holding my mom's hand. I didn't know what was going on around me; I didn't care. Finally, someone grabbed me and dragged me from the lobby, leaving my family and soul behind.

Chapter One: The Cure

THE SUN BEAMED in on my bed as I stiffly moved my arm over my forehead. I squinted up and saw blurry dots as I slowly opened my eyes wider. I gasped for air and felt hot tears rushing down my face as I remembered the dream. The day of my mother and father's deaths always haunted my dreams. I sat up slowly as I reached for my necklace and grasped it tightly. My last gift from my father, and I wore it every day. It was a comfort to hold it in my hands.

I had no one to count on; my parents hadn't kept in touch with any family members after they married. It was just me, with the memories of my family, alone in a big house. I was an only child, but at times like this, I always wished that I had someone to mourn with. As time moved on, you heal. Not always fast, but you heal. I healed alone and without the help of others. That made things harder.

As the months went on, people changed. It was no longer foreign when students went missing from school. Parents built safe houses for themselves and their children, so they would not get the disease. I knew if my family was still whole, I would be hidden away too. My parents had decided to move away to a safe house two weeks before they died. I didn't know where they had planned to take me, so there I was. Some students were taken out of school, but for me, I didn't see the point of college when my parents were dead and the world was soon to follow. The world was pure madness, but I was inside my own personal hell to notice the damage outside. I sat staring at the wall, as I often did after the reoccurring dream of their death. I stiffly got up and walked through the empty house. I was old enough to live alone, and I didn't want anyone's company. This way, I didn't have to be close to anyone, because when they died, I knew I would feel this pain again.

For a while, I didn't speak to anyone. I never opened the door when people brought me things as I grieved. I always believed the disease was contracted from human contact, but I knew better now. I didn't know how people had gotten the disease, but I did know that it started here in my town with Isaac. My father told me many things about the disease, but I tried not to think back to them too much because each memory was clouded with sadness. Eventually I spoke to Kaley. Kaley let me take my time, and I was grateful for that. She was there the day my parents died six months ago, hugging me until the paramedics took them away. She'd been there for me ever since. Thankfully, she stayed in town and went to the beauty school down the street. She understood me and knew that it wasn't easy to get over death. Her father had died when she was nine, and she didn't look at me sad and miserable like most people did.

People were afraid of me. Many people turned their heads whenever they saw me at the grocery store, which was the only time I ever went outside. Many of my friends lost all communications with me as soon as my parents died. Maybe they thought they could catch the disease through the phone or by holding their stare too long with me.

Masks were mandatory out in public; I saw this in the newspaper, and wore one when I went shopping. Since we didn't know how the disease was spread, another unspoken rule was no human contact involving touch. We were all so paranoid, it seemed as if we never wanted to come with in two feet of each other.

Once while I was shopping, a man fell to his knees, screaming when he discovered his daughter had a bruise forming on her leg. He knew it wasn't just any old scrape of the knee, because the lump underneath it told its own story. I watched as a sound blared through the store. Red lights flicked on and off as officials took the little girl from her father. Screaming all the way out of the store as she was taken to the hospital.

I stopped watching the news, so I didn't know what the death toll was anymore, but fear was spreading.

Ding-dong, I didn't even have to wonder who it was. Sometimes I didn't answer when it rang, but that never bothered Kaley. She would just climb through the window. I spent most of my time in my room, or in my father's office. At first, I stayed away from his office, but eventually I saw no reason in hiding from it. He called it a lab, but to me, it was nothing more than a lounge area.

I opened the door and my best friend walked in freely. Her red flaming hair was pulled back into a ponytail. Her freckles made her appear younger than her eighteen years. She was tall and slender with blue eyes that I had always envied next to my hazel ones.

"Well, someone decided to actually move today." She smiled sharply at me. "Get ready." She threw a leather jacket onto the couch. "You're in for a party. The whole town will be there, and you need a boy." She looked me up and down judgmentally. "Definitely."

I groaned. "I don't need a boy, nor do I need to go to a party. I'm not feeling up to it. I don't want to be around them, anyway. Nobody is cautious and it's ridiculous." I flopped down onto the couch, sounding like my mother once did. That stung.

"Honey, you need a pick me up. Plus, it's a big, big day. You won't believe what's going on!" She hesitated and was annoyed when I didn't ask her to clarify, so she continued. "Just go for me then, you can help *me* find a guy."

"What happened to Riley, or Greg, or Joseph?" I muttered without expecting an answer. She answered anyway. "Oh, they were just boy toys. You know how that goes." She hesitated, "Well, don't you want to know what today is all about?" She tried again.

I was not up for her tricks, so I decided to ask, only to please her.

"I'm so glad you asked," she smirked rudely, "the whole town will be in the square because they've found a cure!" She squealed.

"A cure, or the cure?" I asked sarcastically. "Don't look at me that way," I remarked at her look of disappointment. "You don't honestly believe they've found a cure." How could they? My father wasn't alive to have found the cure.

"Lena, maybe I'm wrong. Come out and let me prove it," she said nonchalantly, but I knew her motive. I began shaking my head feverishly. "It'll be a party, a town party. It will be so much fun, just give it a chance. What if the cure is real and solves everything. People are dying to see you." I stared in astonishment.

"Uh, Kaley, who would be dying to see me?" I didn't wait for an answer. "No one. If they wanted to see me, they could come here," I told her in defiance. I was a little curious as to how someone even found the cure, but I didn't want to show her that I cared at all.

"No one wants to come because you're so grouchy," she said as I scowled. "Come on, cheer up," she nagged.

I glanced at her. I didn't want to go out, but I needed to try to keep the only friend I had. Plus, I needed to know what was going on. Had someone stolen my dad's findings for the cure? She could tell that I was contemplating it because her face broke into a large grin. I couldn't help but feel a little excited.

"Fine. I think this cure thing is nonsense, but work your magic on me, Kaley. I haven't put makeup on in about a year." She squealed in exhilaration, and I rolled my eyes.

***

We walked the two blocks to the town square, with Kaley chattering away as we walked. All of our town meetings were located there, and I hadn't attended one in so long, I had forgotten how huge the square was. I was startled to see that the entire town was in attendance. At town meetings, not everyone was always there, like me, but for the cure everyone came out, including me.

I searched for a familiar face. The square looked exactly the same as it once did. The trees were beautiful with bright colors and leaves were turning orange, which meant my favorite time of year was here. The square was a large open space that everyone was welcome to visit. I couldn't help but feel that I didn't belong there somehow. There were shops all around the square, and I spotted one of my favorite places. My mother and I used to walk there for pastries almost every week. I wanted to peek inside the bakery. I would be able to feel some sort of reassurance that my mother was real. We went there in the past, but I didn't want to remember that I was alone without her.

I turned my back to the bakery and looked around the square once more. The lamppost surrounding the square was already turned on, as the sun was slowly beginning to set.

Music blared from all directions, and normally I would have loved to dance, but not anymore. Even Max, the boy from next door, who stayed secluded inside like me, was there. We were in the same class my sophomore year, but he dropped out to stay home. He was more frightened of catching the disease than my mother had been, and that was saying something. But my mother caught the disease, and we didn't. Tears welled in my eyes, but I pushed the thoughts from my mind.

Max waved in my direction, but stayed on the edge of the square, close to the parking lot. I waved back as enthusiastic as possible back to him, and he looked down immediately.

The Fourth of July fireworks were held at the square every year, as were most parties. I never attended the block parties. Kaley was all for the party scene, but I was never one for that.

Kaley immediately started searching the humongous crowd of people for a cute boy. She had always been so wrapped around the fact that she needed a boy to be happy, but I would never live that way. The sudden death of my parents taught me that I didn't need anyone to be happy.

My old friends, Caleb and Julian, waved to me, and I threw a stiff hand up. I was not in the mood to be around all the people who probably assumed I was pathetic. Katherine, a chunky brunette, stepped in front of us, blocking our path and only spoke to Kaley. She threw in a hello to me, but I was sure it was because she didn't want to make Kaley angry. I just looked at her blankly. I wasn't a big fan of Katherine. She used to spread rumors about everyone, and eventually one about me, and I wasn't so forgiving anymore or willing to forget. When she moved out of the way, Kaley grabbed my arm in an unbearable grip.

"Oh, my lord, look, Trevor is here. Why did he have to come? He doesn't care if there's a cure." Before I was able to tell her "neither do you," a dark-haired, lanky boy walked up to Kaley. He strode toward her, while swiping his hair to the side to show off in front of Kaley. I felt her grip on me tighten, and I rolled my eyes in exasperation.

"Hey, beautiful. Want to dance?" he asked her as soon as he approached us, without as much as looking at me. She didn't bother to ask me if I would be okay alone before she agreed to go. Without looking back, she followed him to the dance floor.

I stood quietly on the edge of the sidewalk, just like Max. Suddenly, I felt completely out of place. I looked down at my outfit; I was dressed in my black lace dress with my jean jacket over it. I wore my black combat boots that were completely out of place, but still cute for the look I wanted, which was "stay the hell away." This was a mistake. I was pushing it. I was not ready to go out. I grabbed my necklace and closed my eyes. I started to slow my breathing by imagining that my dad was giving me this necklace for the first time. I did this every time I started to panic. I slowly calmed down and started listening to the music. I swayed a little to compose myself and slowly opened my eyes.

I had the oddest feeling that someone was watching me, so I looked around, but nobody seemed to care that I was there anyway. It was probably in my head, because I wasn't used to being out anymore. My imaginary audience, I supposed. I hadn't been out in so long.

I looked to the dance floor and smiled as I saw Kaley dancing perfectly to the music. Then laughed out loud at the simplicity of it all as she kissed the new boy as he touched the small of her back. Well, I knew the disease didn't spread like mono because Kaley would be the first dead. She kissed plenty of boys before the disease began to destroy lives, and she hadn't changed a bit since it started spreading like wild fire. Kaley was never careful. She always did things so hastily, and I could never do it. Either I wasn't bold enough, or just never wanted a connection to anyone that way.

I decided to stay put where I stood. Everyone was so wrapped up in their own conversations I didn't think anyone had noticed my arrival, like they noticed Kaley. Suddenly, I wished someone would have asked me to dance, or even talked to me because I felt alone. My demeanor was always telling people to stay away, but maybe I needed something to snap me out of my funk. When was this cure coming anyway? It was already 8:00 and some people liked to sleep. Well, people who didn't have a life liked to sleep.

I looked down, and I really did feel ridiculous. Kaley had curled my hair and put a waterfall braid through it to give it flare, but not one boy had stared at me, which didn't bother me. Well, that was a lie. I was only bothered because I wished someone would notice that I was drowning in my own sadness, and I needed a friend. It was not a bad thing to feel alone, but sometimes you needed someone to notice how upset you were.

Sometimes I wished Kaley would talk to me or just try to understand me, but she just talked about shallow, basic things. I could blab about books all day or something complex, but she would rather chat about her boys. I would like to talk about my parents, but she always changed the subject. Maybe she thought it was good for me to not mention them or maybe she couldn't handle it. Maybe she remembered that night as vividly as I did, and she couldn't face the demons so it was easier to not talk about it at all.

As I scanned the crowd again, I noticed a boy starting at me intently. I eyed the ground and felt the blood rushing straight to my face. I looked up slowly to meet his face again, but he was gone. Maybe it was just my imagination, because nobody would look at me. I mentally hit myself for seeing things now.

Someone appeared out of nowhere and grabbed my hips. I jumped in place and looked up to see a boy with blond hair, who was tall and lean. I couldn't place him until he spoke.

"Hey, darling." Eric, he was the biggest jerk in school. I couldn't help but scowl at him.

"Can I help you?" I asked as calmly as possible.

"Oh. Lena, is that you?" He uttered in surprise. "I totally thought you were someone else. You know, everyone thought you'd be up in your house still." He looked me up and down in a way that made me uncomfortable. "Wow. Nice to know that depression suited you." He winked as he backed away. I was sure he felt my eyes wanting to burn the flesh off his face.

"Yes. Depression does many of us well. Now I'm not afraid to kill people because I have nothing to lose." A look of shock spread across his face as his mouth fell open. He threw up his hands as if to say sorry. He left quickly, and I wanted to laugh. *That's right, tell your friends, stay away from me.* Although I wanted to be out of my funk, I didn't want it to be with his kind of people. The jerk kind who Kaley so desperately wanted to be around.

A loud honking sound broke me from my thoughts. A large limo approached the square, and I was reminded why I even bothered coming. To see if the cure was real or just a big hoax. The limo stopped abruptly, followed by about a dozen vans for the local cable stations. They all gathered outside with their equipment. Flashes of cameras erupted all around me as a man with a black suit and cap stepped out to open the doors for his passengers. A man and a younger boy stepped out and remained standing. The boy was broad, with a bitter expression on his face. His lips stayed in a tight line, and he looked as if he could crush someone at any moment. His hair was a dark brown, and his eyes seemed to be pitiless black holes. The man beside him was calmer. Cameras started flashing as they finally began walking. The man held the gazes of each person as he passed. He had brown hair as well, but his blue eyes sparkled. He wore a long white coat that reminded me of what my father wore when he was in his office at work on a new experiment. I couldn't place him, but he looked familiar.

The music had stopped so abruptly I didn't even notice how quiet the crowd was until I turned to see that no one was moving anymore. With each flash of the cameras, I felt sicker than the last. I was so nervous and anxious to know if the cure was real. It was hard to see after a while, but I finally recognized the strange boy with the hardened face. His name was Joseph. He dated Kaley for a year or so, but who could remember, and they broke up just before she began dating Seth. Joseph had disappeared from the neighborhood about three weeks ago after he contracted the disease from his mother. His mother had died six days before he disappeared. Many theorized that he killed himself.

Joseph always had rudeness about him, but now he was just cold. Maybe they brought him back to life so he could suffer more, I wasn't really sure. Just as I tried to decide why he was there, the man in the white coat cleared his throat when mics were placed on his shirt and Joseph's. They reached the very center of the square. Everyone seemed anxious to hear what he had to say. The crowd turned to him like soldiers.

"My name is Dr. Ravana. This here is my friend, Joseph, and it is my understanding that this young man lived among you almost three weeks ago. I found Joseph wandering aimlessly, howling from the pain he was in one night as I left the hospital. He'd been thrashing about among the trashcans. We took him to surgery right away and were about to cut off his arm because of the rot, but then I found the cure." He paused for dramatic effect before continuing. What a show he put on, I snickered to myself. "There have been new advances in technology, as we all know. This recent advance has been something my partner and I had spent time working on." I felt a pinch of pain, and I realized why I knew this man

This was the doctor who worked with my father as his partner to find a cure for the disease. I shivered because this must have been the finding that my father had come up with before his death. It quickly came back to me as I remembered passing him many times in the hallway of my house. I was a ruthlessly angry teenager and never paid much mind to my father's rants of finding the cure for cancer. When I was older, I paid more attention to his rants and saw the importance of his work.

My father was the leading man of the disease control. He worked daily, abandoning his family for the greater good. He used to bring rats home with him, which scared my mother. He would take them to his secured area in the house that he liked to call his lab. In it, he would put strands of Dermadecatis inside the rats to infect them and then he would try to find the cure for the disease. He believed that if he could find one for an animal, then he could find the cure for a human.

"Through the past week, Joseph has been something of a dummy for us." He laughed, but Joseph looked passively into the crowd. Dr. Ravana lifted a small, long block of metal into the air. "This is a chip that doctors will insert into any contaminated arm, leg, hip, you name it. In this case, we put the chip into Joseph's arm. The chip grows into this robotic arm." He clicked a button on the chip and a large arm expanded before us as the crowd all stopped breathing as a whole. "And it clears the disease away. In a month or two, you are back to normal. Completely safe, my friends." He waved to the crowd as if he were king. "I have finally found the cure for this disease and it is here. Now, Joseph, 'The Black Sickness' began in your arm, but show them it now."

Joseph obeyed without a second's hesitation. He lifted his sleeve to reveal completely normal, clear skin. I gasped along with half the crowd, and some people broke off in cheers. But, what was the catch? Did it turn you into some cold person? Joseph looked so angry, but suddenly, as if reading my thoughts, he smiled. His smile was genuine as if he had waited for this moment of triumph for a while.

Dr. Ravana continued, "You see, ladies and gentlemen, the cure is before you. Any questions?"

The crowd broke out in an uproar. Questions were being yelled out from every direction, but none addressed my main concern—what exactly was the cure?

Finally, Dr. Ravana raised his hand to silence the crowd. "Settle down, settle down. I will answer questions one at a time." The crowd was silenced, and he pointed to an older man in the front whose hand was raised high.

The older man cleared his throat, and the whole square was silent with anticipation.

"I have two questions. One is how do we afford this? People like us?" he asked calmly. "But my main question is, what exactly happens when that thing is in us?" He threw his hand toward the chip in Dr. Ravana's hand.

"This cure does not come with a cost. This is a guarantee. Wherever the site of the wounds are, we insert this chip." He clicked the robotic arm and it returned to the former chip. He held up the long silver chip and showed it to the crowd. We all gasped in anticipation. I stood frozen. "This chip will go in and clean out the entire wound or wounds, then it expands and serves as the arm, leg or anything that was rotting. It is like a robotic arm, but not. The chip will act as tissue and will grow as skin. It is a very safe procedure; the chip however, will reside in you forever. But at no cost."

Shouts for new questions startled me, and I listened intently to their shouts. Finally, Dr. Ravana picked a speaker, and it was a young boy. His voice shook. "Is there anymore successes with your cure?"

"Oh yes," Dr. Ravana said. "They are in recovery right now, but Joseph was the only one who could come with me tonight."

More shouting erupted as the flashes of the cameras blinded me.

"Ah yes," he said as he pointed at me. I jumped in place as I heard a voice behind me. I turned to find a girl with black hair and the blackest of eyes I had ever seen, even blacker than Joseph's.

"How do we stop the disease?" It was a simple question, but it had so much strength within it. I froze in place, and I seemed to feel the whole audience shake as I was.

"My dear. What is your name?"

"Cle—" She cleared her throat. "My name is Clementine."

"Well, Clementine. No one knows, and that isn't the point. The point is I have found a way to let you all survive if you do find yourself with the disease."

She looked down quickly, but not before she glared into my eyes. I turned as fast as I could from her so I wouldn't meet her gaze again.

"Any more questions?" Dr. Ravana asked quickly. The reporters began shouting out things. One caught my ear, and I felt tears well up. "What do you think of the death of your partner?"

Dr. Ravana smiled deeply, pointed to the man and responded in a voice so cool I felt as if my ears should be covered as if I were a child. "My partner was a good man. He wanted the same things I did. His death was a tragic mistake. I don't think it had anything to do with what we have done for years. I was asked to work with Dr. Alona for the sake of society." All faces turned to me, and I felt like I wanted to shrink back into my skin and hide there.

"We still don't know how the disease is contracted, but he left me to possess the greatest gift. Dr. Alona gave the cure plans to me, and this is what is in front of you all. The hope of the world is in this technology. We have to now find a way to prevent the disease from being contracted, but that starts with understanding its origin."

Silence was all around me, and I could hear reporters in hushed voices speak about the appearance of a doctor in such a small town. I could hear others speaking about the town being the origin of the disease. I heard the dreaded name Isaac many times. Some seemed to blame Isaac for bringing the disease.

In my haze, I heard a new question. "Doctor, are there any dangerous side effects?"

"Well, let Joseph be the speaker on this one." He pointed to Joseph, and Joseph sulked forward. The doctor patted him on the back and then stepped backward with a look of relief on his face.

"Side effects you asked about. I have to say I feel freedom. If the disease were to come back somehow, the chip would roam through the body to find it. That is another reason the chip should stay within us who receive the cure." He scanned the crowd. "I feel more strength than I have ever before. I feel like I have a clearer head. As you see, there are only good side effects. I did not get sick from the cure. The disease was the part of this that was the worst." Joseph stepped back without another word.

The doctor approached the crowd, smiling brightly. "Any other questions?"

"Can we save the ones who have died?" It was Max. His voice carried through the crowd with a chill. I felt my heart swim with hope. Hope I knew Max was feeling for his mother to return from the dead.

"We cannot my, dear boy. We must mourn the ones who have left us." He hung his head, and I felt my face scrunch up.

After a moment of silence, a voice spoke up.

"Is this chip going to be something that can alter our behavior?" His voice was crisp and beautiful. I searched longingly in the crowd. I couldn't see the face.

"I can hear a voice, but I can't see a face," Dr. Ravana said in a slightly cracked voice.

I didn't understand this new fear in his voice, but before I could think anything more of it, the new voice spoke again. "I don't think that matters." There was a chuckle, and Dr. Ravana's face grew grave.

"Well, faceless man," he said in a sinister way. I felt a chill spread down my arms. "There is no altering of personality. Everything is under control. As Joseph said, he is freer than he was before the disease."

"Perfect." The voice spoke again, and I could hear the hint of a smile. Dr. Ravana looked outraged. He slowly regained composure and smiled once more. I searched the crowd for the faceless man, but there were too many people in the crowd for me to find him. Everyone searched with me, but it seemed as if he were never there.

Every one remained silent. I wanted to scream. Why would we all trust a man who just came off the street in a white doctor's outfit and with no payment? I wasn't buying it. My father told me not to trust just anything when it came to this, but then again, Dr. Ravana worked with my father. What if my father had created this or at least left this information with him. He would have wanted me to trust him. I looked behind me to find the angry girl, but she was gone. I heard shouts of excitement and startled. I turned to find the doctor holding the chip in victory. Many were jumping up and down, and I couldn't bring myself to be happy about it. I looked up to see Joseph still standing in place, as frozen as ever. I could have sworn I saw a flicker of red within his eyes as he stared intently at the crowd.

Dr. Ravana scanned the crowd as he waited for questions. His gaze grazed over me, but quickly retreated back to my face. Recognition seemed to register over his and a panicked look filled his features. Maybe he remembered that I was his partner's daughter, but that didn't explain his fear. He resumed back to his stiff posture as if he had never seen me.

He stared into the distance as he quickly trilled, "If there are no more questions, I must be getting on my way. Everyone have a wonderful party. Goodnight." He backed away in a swift motion and into the limo that he arrived in. It drove away while the reporters crowded around the car, shouting more questions. Most of the reporters fumbled into their vans to follow the limo while some reporting crews stayed to film our small town. Joseph stayed behind and smiled to the crowd as he walked down to them. Noise exploded around me and everyone was so happy to have found a cure, but I had an uneasy feeling that there was something very wrong. I had the strangest feeling that Dr. Ravana was someone to fear and someone who could not be trusted. I didn't know why I felt this way, but I had learned to trust my feelings.

Antidote

Chapter Two: The Reunion

AS THE CROWD moved away and went back to their party, I had the oddest feeling that I was being watched again. I glanced around. I didn't see anyone, but I still couldn't get over the feeling. I found myself staring after the parents and grandparents as they departed the square. I caught some of their conversations of concern for this chip and that they didn't want their children to be reckless tonight. The old man who spoke first at our press conference, was shaking his fists in the air in disbelief.

All around me, I could see that my former classmates seemed to accept the cure extremely fast. I wasn't ready to accept it just yet. I needed more information and answers. I wanted to join the conversations of those older people because they were reasonable. I didn't need to commit more social suicide, though.

I walked to the food table and picked up the laden with cucumber salad, but I couldn't eat. I only went over because I had nothing else to do since I decided against walking home with concerned parents. Kaley was still swaying her hips against the dark-haired boy she probably didn't like, and I was still alone. Now all the parents had left and it was a sea of teenagers.

I caught a glimpse of Max attempting to dance by moving various body parts, but it looked as if he was more interested in joining conversations that didn't include him. He normally would never act this way, but considering that the cure was out, he must have been excited. I couldn't help but feel jealous. Everyone seemed to be accepting everyone else now, and I was still alone. I began to feel as if I should just walk home or at least sit down somewhere when the same eerie feeling of being watched swept over me again. I glanced around to the side of the table where cheesecake was and stopped.

I saw him. The boy I thought was staring at me was real, only this time I was doing the gawking. The boy was not looking at me, but off in the distance instead. I hadn't seen him in the crowd. I wanted to approach him, but I was shy. His brown hair flowed past his ears in wavy forms and almost shimmered in the moonlight. He was broad and wore combat boots that made him look like he was going on a hard voyage. I felt my blood boiling inside my body and I didn't know why.

Then he turned his face, and I could see everything about him, the square shape of his face and the way his brown eyes seemed to glisten in the night's sky. His angular jaw made him look severe, but his eyes were soft. He met my gaze and his mouth spread into a wide grin. That's when embarrassment flooded through me. I knew this boy.

He still was a dream, an impossible, unattainable dream. He wore the same leather jacket he wore the last time I saw him, which happened to be one of the most embarrassing times of my life. One day he was there and perfect, the next he moved away without a word.

We met in English class, and he'd asked me out on a date. I was shocked, because he didn't date anyone in our school. It was rumored that he thought none of us were good enough for him. Of course I told Kaley, who of course told everyone she knew. No one believed me; they laughed at me. Katherine especially got a kick out of it all, and the laughter only got louder because he had completely tricked me. He ditched the following day.

His name was Jared. I never remembered his last name, and I was too ashamed to ask around. It was as if he never really existed. I preferred it that way. He did ask me out, but he didn't show up the next day. I liked to tell myself that he had died. He fell in a ditch, but no one ever recovered his body. That was cruel of me to think, but it was cruel to be stood up as well.

I couldn't deal with humiliation again, so I turned swiftly on my heel and walked away quickly. I didn't hear any footsteps behind me over the music, but I was sure he could care less if he saw me again. That's when a hand tapped my shoulder.

I turned slowly, and there he was. I faced him as he smiled again, which made my heart ache a little, but I kept a stern look.

"Lena?" My gaze met his, and his face was hard and cold. Maybe not, but that's how I wanted to picture it. "Do you remember me?" Jared asked as if he actually wanted to know.

I just looked past him and nodded briskly. I didn't want to be rude, but he really had hurt my feelings. "Yes, I remember you, Jared." I wanted to say how could I forget, but I decided against it. "How have you been?" I asked.

"I've been great. I'm glad you know my name," he remarked sarcastically. "How are you doing?"

"Perfect. Why are you talking to me?" I asked as rudely as I could.

His face fell, and he looked sincerely hurt. Good. He seemed to be looking for something to say, so I turned to walk away from him. I didn't need lies in my life anymore. I didn't look behind me when he yelled my name. That could have just been the music I was hearing, because I was sure he didn't care. I hated him. I hated everyone and everything.

I ran up the garden way along the square that led straight to my house. I looked behind me and gasped to see Jared close on my heels. He followed me. I couldn't help but feel afraid that he had trailed behind me. He wasn't even out of breath like I was. I didn't even notice that tears were rolling down my face. His showed remorse and sadness. But he didn't care for me, just like nobody else did either.

"Lena, Stop!" he called. Not wanting him to follow me all the way to my house. I paused in my escape.

I crossed my hands over my chest and demanded, "What?"

"Lena, I am sorry that I left and stood you up. I wouldn't have done it on purpose. I really had to leave town. I left for the good of everyone, or so I thought." His face was full of disappointment in himself. "Lena, let me make it up to you. I know you've had a hard time recently, so let me help you."

"How do you know that I'm having a hard time?" I asked in disbelief.

"Our dads were friends." He looked into my eyes and said quietly, "I'm so sorry for your loss. I didn't even know he was your father when we met." He looked away from me.

I let that sink in, but I was still angry. In some ways I was jealous. I never got to see my father. I wondered if Jared knew my father more than I did.

"Well," I said, in an attempt to change the subject, "why are you back?"

He looked at me for a long second, and said, "I wanted to make sure I could finish what I started."

"What does that mean?" I asked him.

"It means I will make sure nobody else gets hurt on my accord." Although he was serious, he ended with a genuine smile. He seemed to be thinking thoughtfully about everything he said, but he must have a motive for being there. He just didn't want to tell me. Why would he tell me, anyway? It's not as if he owed me anything. All he did was stand me up.

"Jared, it's been nice talking, but I should get back to Kaley. She's probably waiting for me." That was a lie, but I felt sick and I didn't want to be around him any longer. Even if he was the cutest boy or the boy I dreamed about, more than I should, it didn't erase the past. He scoffed and a sour look came upon his face. He bowed arrogantly and walked away. I stood frozen on the sidewalk. Was he mocking me when he asked for my forgiveness? I would never cry in front of a boy, or anyone, for that matter, again.

I returned to the party, only to tell Kaley that I was going home to bed. As I reached Kaley and her dance partner, a bright light erupted from the sky. I could feel heat radiating from the green light.

Then there was a flash of darkness, followed by screams. Everyone was frantically running, but I stood in place with fear. Each person that was surrounding me ran into me and shoved me backward, but I didn't care. I was being transported back in time to when my mother and father were being killed, and I let out a frustrated groan as I closed my eyes. I couldn't deal with this. I covered my ears as a horrible screeching sound took place. It sounded as if metal was scraping together. The creaking sound crept closer to where I stood frozen. I turned my head slightly to see red dots approaching me. I wanted to run, but my feet were glued to the ground. I heard a whisper in my ear, "Lena, do you know that you are in danger?" he asked into my ear almost seductively, and I wanted to slap him in the face. His voice sounded just like the magical voice asking questions to Dr. Ravana. He whispered even softer, "Run, get out of here. They have come for you."

I didn't need to see to know whose voice it was. Jared lurched me forward with a shove that nearly knocked me to the ground, and he pulled me to reality. I weaved through the crowd and a whoosh of wind soared past me. A pair of hands covered my eyes, and I was frantic until I heard him again. "Stand still. If you want to die, then keep running that way. Follow me, listen to me, and you won't die." He uncovered my eyes and then I heard it. The sound was unnatural. A loud screech came out of something in front of me. It didn't sound human. I was being dragged into a run.

The lights did not return, but I felt weightless as we ran farther away. We were running up the garden way when he caught hold of my arms and pulled me around to face him. "Next time, you should wait to follow me instead of attempting to make your own way into the crowd." His look was as if he were looking at a child and anger surged through me.

"Who the hell are you to tell me what I can and can't do? You shoved me forward? What are you to me, anyway? If they want me, let them have me," I screamed, and his face turned into a sadistic smile.

"What use will you be to the world then? I'm on strict orders, but obviously you are as useless as you look." I felt my cheeks burn as it always did when I felt angry, and I balled up my fists.

"Well, screw your orders. I'm not helping you," I said defiantly. "What happened to the nice guy saying sorry? Was that bullshit?" I arrogantly bowed as he did before.

He laughed, and I wanted to thump him. "Helping me? I'm helping you, not the other way around. Can't you see? They are going to kill you unless you get out of here, and guess who can help you? Guess who has all of the things that could save your life?" He didn't have to wait for me to answer, because it was him. He walked closer to me and leaned down. "He is gone." He sneered. I felt my face turn red in frustration, but I pushed my anger aside.

"What was after me just now?" I asked angrily.

"It isn't safe for you to know the truth. Your mind is your own for now. Let's keep it that way. Trust me. Then maybe you won't die. But if you want to call the shots again, then get going now. You won't make it two miles, and they will find you and kill you, or worse, control you." He continued walking, and I looked behind me. There was smoke coming from the square. Should I turn back and save the others, or save my own skin? I didn't know how to save the others.

I ran after him and asked quietly so only he could hear, "Why should I trust you?"

He looked down on me, and I felt so small. "Who else is there to trust? I'm here, I will help you, and I will take care of you. Your father trusted me. Isn't that enough for you?" The anger in his voice had dissipated a little until he spoke again. "No one else wants to deal with your shit, anyway."

I clenched my fist, but I had to admit that did it for me. If my father trusted him, then I should trust Jared, too. I nodded stiffly, and he led me through the trees and into the pitch-black night.

Chapter Three: Trust

THE DARKNESS DID not stop as we ran to my house. As we reached the driveway, he pulled out a big, black cell phone that didn't look normal in size or style. It didn't have the fancy holograms like I had on mine. It looked more like a walkie-talkie than anything. I wanted to laugh, but it was not the time at all for that. Even if he was a jerk, he was saving me in a way I couldn't do for myself. Without him, I would be dead, trying to help Kaley, or even Max.

My heart began to sink as I thought of Kaley on the street covered with a sheet. I didn't want to see any more death. I didn't want to see Max dead either. He had lost so much, and he was afraid like me. I imagined him in a corner, panicking. I had to get back to them somehow.

He caught me staring suspiciously at his phone, and said, "It's untraceable." He didn't smile. I wondered if he hated me, because I was rude whenever he tried to be nice. Then again he could have been mocking me and that would show he wasn't kind at all. I chose the latter. He wasn't a nice guy, and he proved that a long time ago. He punched a long string of numbers into the phone, more than any other standard number. I watched his fingers sweep across the screen. I admired how even in a tragedy, his hands stayed still, never shaking or faltering. He spoke quietly, but I could hear him. "Gabe, it's time." Someone responded on the other end, and I watched him. I felt my heart quicken as I watched the way he nodded as if the other person could see him. He caught my glance and gave a smirk. I scowled at myself; I couldn't be wrapped up in him. Jared nodded once more and hung up the phone.

"Lena, go in and get your things, but first, we have to go to your dad's office." I stared blankly at him. Why would he need to go to my father's room, and his lab?

"Why? How did you even know that he had an office in this house?" I backed away. There was something he wasn't letting on. "Are you working for someone to find out about my dad?"

He looked frustrated and let out an agitated sigh. "See, you know about things. I'm not the one after you." He smirked in his arrogance. "You would be dead already. No breathing." He leaned forward and touched my face. I flinched away, but his touch left a weird feeling over me. "The ones who are after you wouldn't have given you this much time to run. You can trust me. I will prove it to you eventually. I can prove it to you in your father's room. He left a note for you about me."

"What are you talking about? I would have found it." Maybe it was a trap.

"Not unless you know where to look. Lead the way." He gestured his arm toward the front door, and I didn't move. I heard someone scream close to my house and that got me moving. Jared pushed me through the door because I was too slow.

"Scared, Jared?" I asked with a smile. He didn't respond, but instead, gave me a small shove again.

I stopped suddenly, and he slammed against me. When I stepped on his toes, he let out a gasp. I smirked all the way down the hallway until he tripped me to my surprise. I looked back, and he was whistling while looking the other way. I death stared at him until I was laughing, which seemed to make him smile. I felt my breath take and I looked away fast because the smile he gave me was dizzying. It didn't make any sense to me that he could so easily make me feel weak in the knees.

We reached my father's room, and I opened the door. In the corner sat a desk and to the right of it was a bookcase that reached up to the ceiling.

I threw up my hand as if I said "ta-da" and smirked. "Well, this is it," I told him, but he didn't look surprised or disappointed.

He began to shake his head and than erupted into laughter. "Really? You don't even know? Haven't you ever looked around? Seriously, you need to be adventurous." He shook his head in disappointment and gave me a sour look. I felt myself getting frustrated as he walked to the corner where the desk was and pulled the chair out. He stood atop of it and looked at me one last time. "No idea?" When I didn't respond, he laughed and grabbed the book at the top of the shelf and then the impossible happened.

My dad's "office" transformed. Jared and I flipped upside down without even feeling a thing. I watched as the tabletop turned into a sofa with light blue wallpaper. The pictures of Mom and myself disappeared as his desk flipped into the carpet. The room contained nothing but the sofa, and I scowled. I was disappointed; I really wanted something crazy to happen. I expected potions or something. "This is what you were looking for?" I started to giggle. "How lame. Did you want to lie down? Is this a therapy office?" I giggled frantically and stopped myself when I caught sight of his gaze. He looked frustrated so I stopped talking.

"Done?" he asked in a menacing tone. I looked away. I hated feeling like a child from someone who wasn't that much older than me. "If this were a therapy room, it would be accurately left for you." I felt a sting of pain, but I didn't let it show. I held my head high and walked across the room to where he was standing and held his stare.

He didn't look away for a while, and I felt my heart quicken. He cleared his throat and looked away. "No, he made it this way so if someone got this far, they couldn't get past this." He made a tired sound as he stretched his back. "Go ahead. Walk to the doorway at the end of the couch." He groaned out in frustration.

"This is ridiculous, Jared." I shook my head, and he nudged me to go on.

"Lena, I don't care. I already know what's behind it. I just wanted to let you know. You should probably hurry. They'll realize that you aren't dead yet." He made a spooky face while throwing his hands up into the air like a ghost. I smirked at him.

I walked briskly to the side of the sofa. "Name please." I jumped back. My heart took a leap and I stared gape mouthed at the sound of the strange voice.

"Uh, Lena Alona," I said with a shaky voice. I looked back at Jared, and he shook with laughter. He rolled his eyes as if it was an obvious solution and mouthed the words, *full name*.

So, I scowled, and I tried again with full confidence. "Lena Elizabeth Alona."

"Activate," the voice said.

The wall disappeared completely, and we walked into the room. Jared stood aside so I could explore.

The room with the blue couch seemed to disappear, and was replaced by a room full of bright lights. About sixteen computers lined the walls, and in the center of the room was a giant globe-shaped hologram computer system. Along the wall were many shelves containing bottles of mixtures. I was right about there being potions. I smiled to myself. A large television hung on the right wall.

"What is all this, Jared?" He just nodded at me briskly to continue looking.

I looked at the globe in the center of the room. I peeked in and it was like a crystal ball. There was only a light gray cloudiness in the giant circle. "I don't see anything through this."

He walked over to it. "You tell it what you want to see," he spoke softly. My heart was beating at how sweet he sounded. "This system is under your control now. Your father left this to you. But you know what the funny thing is?" I didn't answer, much to his annoyance, so he continued. "If he really wanted you to have it, how come he never let you know anything?" He smiled in satisfaction as he let that sink in and walked away. "I'm going to guard the door and make sure it's locked." He disappeared from my sight, and I was left feeling useless. He was right, if this was mine then why did I know nothing about it.

I called to him as he walked away. "Where is that note supposed to be anyway, Jared?" He froze, and I smiled. "Ah. There isn't a note, is there?"

"He told me that he left it on the chair, but I didn't see it," he said without facing me.

"Oh, how convenient. You're a liar," I said, and he just smirked.

"How would I know all that I know if I wasn't his friend, his ally?"

I looked at him for a long time. My dad did a terrible job at assigning someone to protect me. Maybe that was what he wanted, someone tough to protect me.

"We can stay here for tonight or we can go. You decide what to do. I'm sure someone will be waiting for us either way. In this room, we can be safe for the night."

"Let me sleep in here. This is where my father was," I told Jared.

"Okay," he said while nodding.

That night I watched Jared. He made me a little nervous. I needed to trust him. It would be hard for me to do that, but I had to get over it. I saw that he was asleep, and once I heard soft snores, I eventually let my eyes shut. I dreamed of my dad and all the things he tried to cure there.

Chapter Four: The Chase

I FOUND MYSELF lying on the floor with a pillow under my head and a blanket over me when I woke up. I didn't have them before and I smiled as I saw Jared had moved slightly from his original resting area. I was unsure if it was morning or night, but I was sure that I had slept a while because I was sore from the floor.

I remembered that we had to leave fast because people might or might not be waiting for us. Who was waiting for us, I didn't know. All I knew was that whoever killed my father was probably out there looking for me. I was still at a loss as to who tried to attack me last night. Jared saved me, even though he didn't seem to like me very much. I didn't understand Jared's motives, because now he got himself in a situation that didn't concern him.

I heard movement on the ground and watched as Jared's eyes popped open as he eyed the TV. His face fell slightly.

I didn't want to turn toward the TV, but I did. What I saw was worse than anything I had seen in my life. In the center of what once was the square, was a huge hole in the ground, where many had been dancing last night. It was as if the entire square simply fell into a huge black hole. The shops by the square were dissolved into dust all around the edges. But that wasn't what took me by surprise. Instead of a death toll on the screen, there was a missing toll. I gasped in shock as I read that seventy-eight people were missing. The entire square was demolished, so the reporters probably couldn't tell if citizens were killed or just missing. The events of last night were too weird. Who caused the square to blow up like that?

Faces popped up all over the screen in a matter of seconds—my neighbors, my classmates, my old friends who were all missing because of me. I knew this was my entire fault, but I couldn't bring myself to accept the fact that someone really wanted me dead. Did they really kill others to get to me, or took them away to bring me to the surface? I was glad to see that Kaley was not on the list, so I gave a sigh of relief. Maybe I should have just turned myself in to whoever wanted me. I didn't bother bringing this up to Jared because he wouldn't have allowed it. After all, he risked his life for mine.

I thought of the green light that surrounded me last night and couldn't shake the feeling that whoever came down to chase me took my friends, too. I remembered the way I felt and the red eyes I saw. A chill ran down my spine. What did they want from my friends or me? I looked to Jared, and he didn't look in the least bit surprised anymore. He stared blankly at the screen and his lips were pressed in a hard-pressed line. He looked so angry that I shuddered when his gaze meet mine briefly.

"We have to get out of here, Lena. They are killing people and taking others," Jared said quickly as he got up.

"Jared, maybe it would be best if I was gone. Then people wouldn't be taken away because of me," I said to him.

"Lena, they would have taken them with or without you. You don't determine the fate of others," he said without looking at me, as if he wanted to hide his face from mine. He shook his head in disapproval. "You should trust me," he said calmly. "I have proven myself to be valuable, so trust me."

"I can't trust you." I sighed softly. "This is very scary for me. Can't you understand that? I'm afraid because I have lost everyone. I don't want to lose myself as well because I trusted you." I hesitated. "How did you know my father?"

He looked annoyed. "I can't tell you here, but be smart and trust me. You're going to understand soon enough. And if you don't want to trust me because I'm tough on you, then you're a coward."

I just shrugged as he stood up. After counting to three, I followed him out. We entered my dad's room again, and before I knew it, Jared dragged me furiously to the floor. Just when I was about to scream in protest, he slapped a hand over my mouth and put a finger to his lips, pointing to the window. There were two shadows that I could see through the curtain. I started to panic, but Jared remained calm. Somehow this made me feel a little less scared.

He crawled on the floor toward the curtain, and I wanted to shout to him to not go near the window, but decided against it because I didn't want to draw attention to him. Jared pulled from his pocket what looked like a giant magnifying glass. In the center of his gadget was something that looked like a mirror. Wires were coming out of the mirror on the back. He held it up toward the window and instantly the glass disappeared. I could see outside and beyond the curtains now. When it finally adjusted, two faces appeared. The first was Joseph Jacobs, the boy with the first cure, and the second was my neighbor, Max Schrubs, the boy who was always afraid.

I sighed and smiled at Jared. He looked at me with a crazy look on his face. I started to get up off the floor, but he slammed me down onto the floor. I gasped for air.

"What are you doing?" I whispered frantically.

"Lena." He shook his head, and I looked in his eyes, confused.

"What is it?" I asked slowly, still whispering.

"I don't think they're here to see if you survived." He looked at me with a meaningful look, but I still was lost.

"Jared, but Max is out there." I searched his eyes for him to agree with me, but he just looked at me in a sad way. It was as if he were feeling sorry for me for believing there was an ounce of goodness in someone.

He looked into my eyes once more and put a finger up to shush me. I took a gulp and laid my head against the cold ground again.

So these were the people after me, but why? They weren't exactly scary in my eyes. Maybe Joseph for his cold demeanor, but Max was not scary in the least. Max tricked me into thinking he was scared, when he was probably watching me from his house. What got me was how belittled I felt by Max wanting to capture me for whatever reason. If you so much as sneezed around him, he ran for cover. Jared looked passively to me and out the window again, but this time, he pulled out what looked like a gun, and I almost screamed.

I had never been within miles of a gun before, but he looked at me with a look so severe I didn't make a sound. Jared pulled the trigger, and I covered my ears. No sound. The boys outside did not move, but instead looked as if they were frozen in place. Jared got up, pulling me with him. He broke into a run.

"I don't understand!" I shouted to him as we ran, and he looked back to silence me before finally answering.

"I froze them into shock. They will stay that way thirty seconds, tops." I was terrified. "We need a car. Now. We have to break out of here before they break the trance," he told me. I led the way to the garage where my dad's black Audi R8 sat.

I slipped into the passenger's seat as he got behind the wheel. The keys were on the dashboard, and as the car roared to life, I began to panic. He looked to me and chuckled when he saw my hands shaking tremendously. "Don't panic," he said softly.

He opened the garage door, and as it rose, I saw three figures blocking our exit. We were trapped. Jared pulled his "gun" out again, and they all froze. With a quick sideways flick of his wrist the three figures flew into the air as if they were statues, out of our way.

He floored it out of the garage, and I caught sight of the house behind us as they moved from their stances. I faced forward and told Jared that they all seemed to have moved. He just laughed, and said, "I know. They will come after us for a little while. They won't go against orders."

"They will still come after us?" I asked in horror. "Who is giving them orders? They aren't working on their own?"

He just chuckled under his breath. "You are the real deal. You have all the answers whether you think so or not. They know that you know. They want to eliminate the threat, and that is you." He laughed. "And no. No one moves on their own anymore."

"Turn around!" I said in disbelief. "Let me tell them that I know nothing, because I don't even know what's going on. They have the wrong girl." A new thought came to my mind. "Take me to who wants me so badly at least."

He didn't as much as slow down as he turned to me slowly, and said, "You are Sebastian Alona's daughter, right?" He didn't want an answer so he continued. "Start acting like it. You're a real wimp." He turned back to the road, and I sat in silence. "As for going to the source, what good is that? You're the only hope." I let that sink in, and I felt a weak happiness, but I let it subside. This meant I was going to have to fight for my life and maybe even save others. I felt fear, but I let that feeling go as well and continued my questionnaire.

"Why is Max with them? He was such a weenie. I can't believe any of this," I said to myself mindlessly. Jared snickered, and I looked over angrily. "This isn't funny!"

He searched the road as he grinned. "You said weenie, kid."

I scowled to the mirror. It was morning. The sun slowly came up, and I relaxed a little because this was my favorite view. I always watched it from my window at home. I found a tiny shred of comfort in that moment, but then I shivered at the thought of what would have happened to me if Jared hadn't come along.

***

A few hours later, I continued to stare out the window. Jared was still driving. I didn't know how he wasn't tired, but he didn't seem to be affected by driving for three hours. No one came after us yet. I was relieved, but I wondered if that meant soon they would.

I stared at him and felt the warmth of the sun on my face. I cleared my throat as he turned to me with full attention. "So, where are you taking me?" I asked.

"Can't tell you. I would have to kill you." He glanced over with a sinister look, and I was unsure if he was kidding or not.

"Oh, funny," I said. When he didn't respond I sat in silence.

What if this was a trick? And what was worse was that I let him trick me. I turned quickly from him. I was such an idiot. He was bad, and I trusted him to come into my house. That was why he didn't kill them; he just put them in a trance. No, that was morbid. Maybe he just really didn't want to kill anyone because, who would want to do that?

"Why can't you tell me?" I questioned defiantly.

"Well, say they had bugged the car? They would know where to go."

"But if they bugged the car, they've probably installed a GPS, too," I told him, but he ignored me and acted as if I didn't speak. I was frightened, and I didn't want to be killed. This boy, the boy who hurt me before, was so mysterious. I couldn't stand the way he made me feel as if I wasn't important and important in the same breath. I was caught up in my thoughts when a huge bang came from the top of the car, breaking the silence.

"What was that?" I turned to Jared, and he twisted to me slowly. His eyes were wide and his face paled noticeably as he panicked. His cool demeanor had fallen.

"They found us. I didn't think they would this soon," he told me quickly and sped the car up to at least 105 miles per hour. He moved the wheel in jagged movements until there was another thud outside.

"What are you doing?" I shrieked. I looked out the window to see a figure on the ground. "Oh, my god. Jared, did you just kill him?"

"Not even close. He's coming back," he said through gritted teeth.

I checked the side mirror and the figure was no longer on the ground. He wasn't even in sight of the mirror anymore. I sighed because we didn't hurt him, but then I saw him. I really saw him. He was standing on the hood of the car. How could anyone ever do this? Jared sped up again, but the boy did not even jolt with the speed increased. Jared slammed on the brakes and quickly sped the car back up, but he didn't budge. He walked slowly toward me on the car. No human could ever do this. Jared tried to get his gun out, but it was too late.

Joseph kicked the window out of the car while it plunged to a stop in the middle of the road. I screamed at the top of my lungs. The window shattered as I shielded my eyes. I felt a sharp pain on my forehead. I uncovered my eyes and opened them to redness. The blood gushing into them blinded me. Suddenly, I felt a hand close around my neck. I felt as if my head would snap off if it were squeezed any harder. I tried to gasp for air, but it was hopeless. I would never be able to take a breath again. I threw my hands to my neck. I clawed at his cold skin as I tried to get his hands off my neck. I could feel myself blacking out, and I didn't know what to do. I started throwing my hands around, attempting to stab him with my nails. I grabbed a piece of glass that landed on my lap to hurt him. Through blinded eyes, I slashed around, but my weapon was quickly ripped from my hands. I couldn't go out without a fight.

Suddenly, someone grabbed my arm, and I felt a stabbing pain. I felt warmth pour down it. Where was Jared? Maybe he made a run for it because he didn't want to lose his life or maybe he joined in? I would die not knowing who killed me. I thrashed and tried to fight the people attacking me. The hand around my neck released me suddenly, and I felt myself drifting off. My eyes went from red to black in a matter of seconds.

Chapter Five: The Treatment

WHEN I RECOVERED consciousness, we were sitting on the side of the road in the car. I looked above me to see Jared holding his shirt over my head. His jacket was still on and zipped up so he wasn't exposed. *He must be bashful*, I thought to myself. He looked panicked, but I didn't think he wanted me to know. I wanted to get up, but I felt as if I were being held to the seat by a block of cement.

"How did you get them to stop?" I asked, dazed.

"I took care of it. Don't worry about it." He looked grimly down at me.

"What's wrong? I feel so dizzy and weak. I can't even get up," I told him.

He didn't answer. Instead, he gazed out the window to the sky and took a deep breath. "Lena, we are going to have to take you to the hospital. Your head is gushing blood, and look at your arm. It's bleeding so profusely I'm surprised you haven't died from blood loss. I hope nobody sees us." He started the engine and drove down the road. The roar of the car countered the drums that were beating inside my head.

"Who would hurt me at a hospital? Do I really need a hospital, anyway?" I tried to lift myself, but Jared put a hand up to block me. I slouched back down. "Just take me to a hospital around here. I'm sure we'll find one." He didn't look at me or answer, so I sat there in silence.

"How far away are we from town?" I asked weakly, my eyes began to shut slightly.

"Don't sleep," he shouted. I jumped, but my eyes still felt heavy. "We must be two miles from town. Hold on, Lena." I felt the car accelerating, but I was too dizzy.

"I wish you weren't hurt this bad. Holland could easily stich you up, but you're losing so much blood." He touched my forehead. A flutter rippled through my stomach. I bit my tongue hard to remind myself Jared wasn't the guy for me. "They got you good. Didn't you think to cover your face?" he shouted angrily.

"Well, excuse me. I've never been in a situation like this before, so no. I didn't think to do much of anything. I did cover my face!" I softly told him, and my eyes were shut once more, but I blinked them open. I could tell my vision was getting fuzzy.

"Well, your eye could have been better than you losing blood!" he railed at me. I wanted to yell how stupid and ignorant that was, but I didn't have the strength. Everything I did was impossibly wrong to him.

We drove down the road until we saw a sign for a hospital. The car was making me woozy. I felt as if I was going to pass out again. We reached the hospital, and he stopped the car far from the entrance. I looked at him as best as I could. How was I going to get there? I would have to crawl for sure. This was a cruel joke.

"How can I get there?" I asked in shock.

"I can't go in with you. People will recognize me, and it's too dangerous right now. Tell the nurse that you were driving alone and you hit a tree with your car and walked here. Hurry in; you're losing too much blood. I wouldn't send you in if it weren't serious."

I didn't answer, I just got out of the car uneasily. Before I shut the door, I looked to him. "Don't leave me, if that's what you're trying to do." I tried to slam the door, but fell against it instead. I began to fall forward, but before I landed on the ground, a pair of hands gripped me tightly. I looked up to see Jared staring at me with his hard eyes. If I weren't so hurt, I could have sworn he had tears building. "Maybe it will be worth the risk," he said soothingly to me.

He gently picked me up, and I leaned my head against him. He walked so fast I didn't even know we entered the building until I felt the cool air from the AC. I heard hushed voices and finally felt a chair beneath me. "You're going to be okay. You have to be." Jared spoke to me softly.

When I looked up to thank Jared, he was rushing through the front door where we had just come. I slumped down in my chair. The waiting room was completely empty, except for two women speaking in hushed voices.

The lady at the front desk with blue glasses, finally looked in my direction and jumped up from her desk. "Oh my, honey, what happened?" The lady with glasses immediately snapped at the nurse she was just speaking to. The nurse was smaller than anyone I had ever seen before, and she wore black scrubs. She rushed forward with a wheelchair. She helped me off the chair and gently into the seat. "We need to see her right away," she told the nurse as she began wheeling me forward.

The nurse smiled suspiciously to me as she pushed me around the corner. I looked behind to see the secretary smiling at me, too. I had an odd, uneasy feeling rush through me, but it quickly subsided as I caught sight of a trail of blood beside me. My arm was hanging from the side of the wheelchair and the line of blood was my own. I felt my head drooping down to the side, and my eyes got blurred with red again. The nurse called on her pager, and instantly a man's voice answered.

"We have another," she said, and I looked to her about to dispute. Another one? There was a stinging in my right arm, and I saw as she pulled away from me that she had a syringe in her hand.

"What is that for?" I protested weakly. Instantly, I felt tired and I closed my eyes. I felt myself drifting off. In my thoughts, I thought I heard her say, "This is for your own good, Lena." But that was just my thoughts playing tricks on me, because I never once told her my name.

***

I awoke to a stark white room with many lights and silence. I didn't feel safe. My forehead tingled, although I wasn't as dizzy anymore. I wanted to get up, somehow I knew I would fall. I glanced around the bed for a call button to get a nurse. To my surprise, there wasn't one.

I gripped the side of the bed, and I realized my clothes were still on. Normally at the hospital, they would put a gown on you, but not there. I wished I had a change of clothes, because I was wearing the same black dress with my jean jacket from the night before. I caught sight of a red bloodstain on my jacket, so I pulled it off instantly only to find that there was blood splattered along my dress as well. I forgot to get anything to change into in my haste to leave this morning.

I got up unsteadily and clung to the side of the bed. When I gained my balance, I made my way to the exit door. I needed to find Jared and get out of there, because this place gave me weird vibes. I reached for the handle and pulled as hard as I could manage in my weakened state. Nothing. The door was locked, and I began to shake with fear. They locked me in from the outside, and then it hit me that this was a trap. Probably assembled by Jared. This was a scheme to get me there to kill me. So I ran to the window and pulled it open, thankful that it opened with ease. I was up too high to climb out. There were too many floors between the ground and myself. I began to hyperventilate because my worst fear was falling to my death, but someone murdering me would be worse. If I climbed to the other room beside me, maybe that door wouldn't be locked.

I stepped over the side of the window and began slowly climbing on the tiny ledge. I sucked in my breath as I felt with my feet that the walkway was slowly getting slimmer. What have I gotten myself into? I stood on my toes while hugging my body to the building. I had white knuckles from how tightly I was grasping the brick wall. I caught sight of my face in the glass portion of the building and saw a large white bandage over my right eyebrow. I looked hideous. There was dried up blood running in streaks all the way down my cheeks. It covered my eyelids. I closed my eyes in horror and recovered fast as a whoosh of wind slightly threw me to the side. I had to keep moving.

I was feeling my heart patter in my ears, but I knew I had to get out of there. The adrenaline coursing through my veins had made my fear of falling seem so petty. I continued until I caught sight of an opening. I pushed on the window, but it didn't budge. I was careful not to look down. I stayed focused and traveled on the wall to the next window. There had to be one that would open. I kept gliding on the ledge until I reached my next hope. I was not sure how I made it that far without falling. I pushed hard on the glass, and it flew open. I lurched forward into the room. I took a deep breath and said thank you internally.

The room was empty and the door was closed. I prayed it was not locked. I walked toward the door when I heard the window slam behind me. The only sound I heard was the pounding in my chest. I ran to the bed and ducked beneath it. The adrenaline in me had dissipated, and I knew I couldn't take the pressure now. I peaked from under the bed to the window and saw that it was wide open and a pair of feet appeared from in front of it with a small thud. My stomach hit the floor, and I stopped breathing as I heard heavy footsteps coming toward the bed. I saw black combat boots closing in on my hiding place, but I remained quiet. The boots stopped at the edge of the bed, and the leather squeaked as the owner squatted, and I saw an all too familiar face peeking at me.

"Hmm, I sure am glad it's just me," Jared said thoughtfully, and I wanted to slap the patronizing look off his face. "Are you crazy? Everyone could see you scaling the building like you were a rock climber. Say someone wanted to kill you? They would've had a clear shot, or you could've died on your own accord. I was sitting in the car, saying, what idiot is doing that? Then I said to myself, who else would be so reckless? And I was right. Thought I would come up and save your ass. Let's go." He stood with ease, and I scowled. Thanking god the lecture was over.

"How did you get here so fast?" I asked curiously.

He pulled out a metal piece and looked at me as if I knew the answer. "Gabe made this. I can scale any building with it, and *voilà*. Here I am. Only bad thing is you can't go back down with it." He frowned at it and didn't wait for me to understand. "Let's go," he added hastily.

He didn't lend me a hand as I slid from under the bed and stood. "Wouldn't have gotten out of the room if I hadn't done that. Thanks for that lecture though." I flipped my hair to be rude, and then he stopped me by placing his hand on my stomach. Again with the butterflies and the weird feeling in the pit of my stomach. He grabbed my chin and studied my face. His gaze normally piercing and cold was kind and soft, and I was oddly afraid that he would move closer. My heart quickened, and I wanted to look away, but his gaze was so captivating I couldn't pry my gaze away. Blood rushed to my cheeks, and I got angry with myself again. *Don't let it show, you idiot.* Then I remembered that my face was covered with blood and would hide any new color to my cheeks.

"Just checking to see what they did." He gave a quick arrogant smile. He must have noticed that my breathing had stopped completely in that moment. "Act normal, and when I say run, you need to run. If I tell you to go without me, you need to do that, too. Okay? Don't try to act strong because, quite frankly, you're not."

"I'm not some weak little girl, okay? Get over yourself. You lead people on and stand them up. I'm not worthless, and I sure as hell don't hurt people." I felt my heart picking up and I gripped my necklace for confidence. There was a bubble that traveled up in my throat almost choking me, and I felt the unshed tears burning behind my eyes.

He stared in amazement and just nodded swiftly. "I was wrong then." He didn't say anything more. He opened the door casually. I wondered if I needed to clean the blood off, but I didn't ask. Jared searched down the hall, and I followed his gaze. There were three boys standing with their backs to us, and they were trying to get into the room that I was just in.

One boy started beating the door, and I realized it was Max. Joseph pushed Max to the side and slammed the door open with his foot. Then there was chaos. Joseph started hollering, and a new face I had never seen, turned slowly to us. His eyes seemed to be glowing, and he started shouting to the others. It all happened so fast, but all I could concentrate on was Jared screaming, "Run!"

My feet took off before my mind could catch up with me. We ran, and all the nurses stopped in place. They didn't seem surprised to see me running and they quickly returned to their duties, except a few who ran after us with the three boys. I didn't recognize any of the nurses, but they seemed to know exactly who I was.

As we approached the elevator doors, Jared pulled out a slingshot and shot a dart to the down button and as we reached it. It opened. Jared frantically hit the first floor button as the others reached the elevator, and just before the door slammed shut, I caught sight of my golden blond-haired enemy. Eric from high school. I gasped for air as we soared down. I stared at Jared, and he didn't look as shaken as I felt. "Does everyone I have ever known have it out for me?" I asked loudly.

He looked down to me, and for a second, I saw a glimpse of remorse. "I shouldn't have come in. You could have handled it alone. I'm so sorry." I stared at him in surprise.

"What are you talking about? I would have died. I wouldn't have known what to do. I would have taken the stairs and been dead by now." As I said the words, I wanted to take it back. The lights went out in the elevator as it froze in place.

"Jared, what is going on?" I started to shake, and I moved my hand to my mouth.

"I don't know," he said slowly.

The floor began to shake uncontrollably, and I looked down and saw light coming in. "I think the floor is going to bust!" I shouted as I gripped his hand before I could stop myself. To my surprise, he squeezed back. I looked down at it in awe.

Then the lights flickered on and the elevator took a plunge down. I started to scream, and if Jared was screaming, I would never have known. This was the end. I looked at Jared. He looked at me with almost a note of disappointment. It might have been because he had to share death with me, so I closed my eyes. My breathing slowed. I focused on each inhale and exhale as the next one could be my last. I didn't scream anymore. I listened to the wind blowing as we flew down in the elevator. Time seemed to move slowly. I knew we were going fast down many stories of floors.

Suddenly, the door chimed open, and I was blinded by light when I opened my eyes and saw the opening to the elevator. Before I knew it, Jared was pulling me behind him, our hands interlocked still. The boys were running from the stairwell. Joseph put his hand up to stop them and sneered. They stopped in place. I caught sight of Max. One moment his eyes were a violent emerald. The next second, they were a golden-brown. They all turned and acted like nothing happened.

I stopped in place and stared at them. Lurching, Jared to a stop as well. What was that? They chased us and just stopped. Jared was roaring at me to keep coming. He let go of my hand to my dismay and ran ahead of me. I took off in a sprint again after him.

We ran all the way to the car, and I frantically jerked the car door open and climbed in. My energy felt renewed as we drove off with the Audi screeching. I felt calmer but not relaxed until we were completely out of sight of the hospital.

"Why did they let us go like that?" My voice shook as I asked him.

"They must know something we don't. Maybe someone else is coming for us," he told me in an agitated voice. I thought it was because I kept asking useless questions, but I was confused. He must want me to know everything. He expected too much of me, and I couldn't help wondering why.

I took this in and tried to feel safe, but I didn't. Since everyone wasn't who they seemed to be, I didn't know if it was wise to let my guard down. My head was tingling again. I didn't want to mention that my body felt as if it were scorching. I looked down and noticed that my arm had turned a pale pink beside the cut that went down my forearm. There were lumps forming all along the cut. I felt my chest tighten in response. I saw my father's face appear, but shook the thought right out.

"What's wrong with their eyes?" I asked Jared to distract myself from how weird I felt.

"You saw that too?" he asked. "I'll have to ask Gabe. He's a genius. He always knows things before I do, and he can figure things out without even seeing them. You'll meet him and Holland soon," he told me with a satisfied smile.

"How will I meet him or her?" I asked puzzled by his smile.

"Well, I'll tell you now, because they seem to catch us either way. If the car were bugged, they would find out anyway. We're going to my safe house."

"Where is it?" I asked in disbelief. I watched the darkness around me and felt drowsy. A safe house, I truly believed I would be safely at one if my family were still together.

"The coast of North Carolina. You can rest. I'm going to find somewhere to sleep because I'm getting tired, too."

"I can drive," I told him excitedly through my sleepiness, because I had loved this car and never was able to drive it.

"No, I appreciate you asking, but you're not in any shape to drive."

"No, I want answers, and I'm not sleeping until I know the truth," I stubbornly added. "This is my dad's car, and if I want to drive it, I will."

"Lena, you must know that there are things I can't explain, and there is something coming bigger than both of us. It's scary, but I will figure this out. Don't worry about it." He ignored what I had said about it being my car, so I crossed my arms angrily.

"What does that even mean? You think I have all the answers, but I can't even help finding things out. I have a right to know. Maybe more than you do since he was my father. I'm not useless, I want to be helpful, so start talking."

"Lena, just don't try to act like you can help until you know what I want to know."

I began biting my nails in exasperation. "So, I'm only useful when you say so. Well, stop the car. I will do this alone."

"Don't be stupid. You'll be out in the open, and what use will you be then?"

"You get out then," I said with a smirk.

"That will be super helpful, and while you're at it, have fun trying to find the safe house." His stare pointed out how foolish I was being.

I let that sink in and gave a frustrated sigh. I calmed down and slowly said, "I don't know what's going on, and you expect me to trust you when I don't even understand what they want with me or from me. I have no knowledge of what my father did, or what he knew, so why am I so damn important?" Truly, I didn't trust Jared. I did know a thing or two about my father's work. But if Jared were really in cahoots with my father, he would know these things, too.

"Maybe this is good. You don't know anything that would get you killed," he told me, but it didn't make me feel any better, but I didn't interrupt. "This could be really good. But the thing is, you do know. You just won't know until the time is right. Or if someone forces it out of you. Not me, of course," he said when a flash of fear crossed my face. "If you're still confused in a few days, I will tell you. But for now, if they were to take you, it's best that you know nothing." I shuddered at the thought of them taking me. But I tried my best not to let it show. "We aren't far from North Carolina, anyway."

"Why North Carolina?" I asked. Curiosity seemed to take the best of me. It had been so long since I got to talk to someone other than Kaley. I hadn't heard from Kaley at all, and I had my cellphone with me. Or rather I did. It was in my jean jacket, which I abandoned.

"My mom's favorite beach trip was when we went to Wilmington. But she died while I was building the safe house. I didn't want to finish it after she died, but

I'm glad I did. I've been protecting two of my best friends there."

"How did she die?" I asked and bit my tongue, immediately regretting it. He didn't respond. So I decided to say the nicest thing I could conjure up about him.

"That is really kind of you to have the house there for your friends." He gave a hint of a smile, but quickly returned to his reserved demeanor.

He was silent, and I looked out the car to the world around me. I felt my breath take.

"Jared, slow down."

"Lena, please, this car is meant to go fast. You can't tell me you don't love speed," he said and laughed, but I felt no humor.

"Where are we?"

"We can't be too far from Texas. Why?" Finally he slowed the car. That was when it all came together.

"Stop the car." When he didn't I shouted louder. "Please."

He stopped, and I stepped out. The smell was disgusting. It smelled as if a fire burned its way through a million bodies. I covered my face with my arm. Jared stepped out, and I looked back to him. "What happened here?" He looked around frantically, and I took a deep breath.

"Lena." He shook his head. "Texas has been deserted for a week now." I looked to the road we were just on and saw many abandoned cars there. We were the only people around for miles. I looked back to the destruction I saw. In the open field, there were bricks from where houses once stood. In the center of the field, a black hole that was strangely similar to the one from my town.

I dropped to my knees. "Why wasn't this shown on the news?" I asked softly.

"This is what happens when the cure is introduced to each town or city."

"The cure did this to people," I said in disbelief. I looked back to him. He still had half his body in the car.

"No, Lena." He got back into the car and shut the door behind him. I sat looking at the destruction around me in horror.

A voice came behind me and I looked up once more to the car. Jared rolled down the window. "Let's go get some rest. We're out in the open, and we might look like this small town soon."

I got up slowly. I saw pictures of Texas, but had never seen it first hand. It was a beautiful place, and now it was gone. Wiped out for miles. I couldn't help but wonder if my town would be the next to look like this.

Chapter Six: The Confusion

WE ARRIVED AT a small hotel on the side of the road. Jared told me we weren't too far from the safe house. It was about six hours away. I wanted to clean up a little. I wanted to wash away what I saw. I had money with me at all times because I kept it in my sock, which was something my dad had told me to always do. I paid for the room. The hotel we stopped at had a small breakfast diner across the street, so we could have breakfast in the morning.

We got our room key from the desk downstairs by two suspicious hotel owners, who didn't speak a word to us but whispered to each other softly. Which was no surprise since I was still covered in blood. We headed back outside and made our way to the steps that took us to the room 206. The wind outside made my eyes water. We walked in silence, and I didn't mind because I was tired as well. I didn't realize just how tired until we climbed the steps. The room has peeling yellow paint with a small bathroom beside the bedroom. The queen-sized bed sat in the middle of the room with a TV facing it. He laughed, and I looked up his tall body to see his face completely unfazed by the bed.

"You take the bed, I take the floor." I was surprised he didn't say the opposite.

Before I could stop myself, I said, "I can't let you sleep on the floor. That's terrible. I'll take the floor."

"Don't be silly." He walked away to the TV while laying down bandages he must have taken from the hospital room. I was struck that he thought to get them for me. He turned the TV set on, and the most peculiar sound erupted from it. The TV focused in and the news channel blared on full blast.

"Just in, a young man by the name of Keaton Rivers has been missing for two days. It appears that he was last seen in a gray sweatshirt with black Nikes. Here is a picture if anyone comes across him." A picture of a redheaded boy holding a soccer trophy appeared on the screen. "Over to you, Elizabeth."

"Hey, John, I have been in charge of the accounts of kidnappings for the past year, and it has came to 6,908 of them. In just one year." She raised an eyebrow before continuing. "It is so odd that there have been such crimes during this time, but people are panicking around the world due to Dermadecatis. But I bear good news. Ever since the cure has come out, there has been an even lower death toll than normal. I'm proud to say that there have been 105 cases of the cure today. There have been so many people saved. It is so won—"

The TV shut off abruptly, and I was so lost in the newscast that I didn't even realize Jared was shaking uncontrollably in the corner.

"What is it?" I asked evenly. He stared off into space. I walked to him, feeling my anger build. "Jared, you have to be honest with me and tell me what you know. You obviously know something I don't. Just talk to me." I swallowed my anger down. "If you talk to me, maybe I can remember things, too." I knew more than I let on. I wanted to open up to him.

"I need some time alone. Just give me some time," he muttered before he got up and walked for the door.

"Wait. Please don't leave me alone. I can't be alone." Tears spilled from my eyes, and I wanted to pinch myself for showing any emotion. I already told myself I wouldn't cry in front of him again.

"You're fine." I felt tears welling up, and he reached for my face. I leaned into it and watched him as the tension faded from his expression. "I won't be far." His touch made my heart pound, and I tried to ignore it. "Bolt the door, and let no one in." He shut the door behind him, and I stared at it. I buried my head in my knees before getting up after him. I opened the window curtain and stared outside. I didn't see him, and I was not sure where he went.

I took a shower while I had some privacy. I closed the door and locked it behind me. I looked in the mirror and saw myself for the second time since the hospital. I let out a loud gasp, because I appeared to be like something from a horror movie. My brunette hair was red with blood in the front. I started laughing alone, which made me feel even crazier. Maybe I was crazy after all I had seen.

I stripped down and got into the shower. The dried up blood had me believe that my skin would be stained red for a while. I really wished I had brought more clothes. I scrubbed my legs with soap as the blood and grime went down the drain. When I got up to my right arm to scrub, I stopped in place and remembered that it wasn't looking right in the car. I didn't want to think of why. I didn't want to believe something like that.

I gently scrubbed and felt a pinch of pain as my skin began peeling from my arm. I jumped back and realized the pink skin around the lumps began to bleed quickly as skin flaked off. I frantically grabbed the bottle to see if the soap was dangerous to use. There was nothing out of the ordinary. I began to tremble because what I saw was not ordinary.

My arm had turned into a bloody mess. The tub turned completely red. I started to scream and held my arm up to my face to look more closely. Black was all around it. I felt a lump in my throat as a shiver ran down my spine. This wasn't happening. Not to me. Not to the one my dad promised would never ever get it. Tears flooded my eyes and flowed down my cheeks. I dropped to my knees in the bloody water as the sea of red spirals went down the drain. I screamed at the top of my lungs, but no one came. I punched uselessly against the tub with my left hand as my right arm lay limply beside my knee. It still bled, and I didn't know what to do about it.

I sobbed as I covered my face with my left arm. I gingerly peeked at my arm again and blinked into focus. I rubbed my eyes for good measure and was astonished. The blood around me had disappeared and I was left with the clear water from the showerhead above, splashing onto the back of my neck. The pale pink color had returned to my arm, and instead of being multiple lumps, there was a large lump in its place. There was no trace of black. I must have hallucinated the whole thing. I looked around the tiny bathroom, crazed. Was it all in my head then?

I shut off the water and stepped out of the bathtub. I grabbed a towel and began to retch as I caught a glimpse of my reflection in the mirror. I leaned forward to look more closely. The bandage around my head was blood red.

I ripped the bandage from my head, and my forehead was a black color just like my arm previously was. I had to be going crazy, and I moved closer to the mirror. I grabbed a washcloth and dampened it with water. I began to dab at it, but the black did not disappear, and so I ran to the bedroom where Jared had laid bandages out before he left in his haste. He still wasn't back from his walk.

I returned back to the bathroom in a hurry and unraveled the bandage from the package. I glanced up to place it on my head and stopped in my tracks. The black was completely gone and my stitches were not bloody. I picked up the old bandage where the blood was just at, but instead it was pale pink from just a little discharge. The blood I just saw was gone. I felt my hands slipping from the edge of the sink and the last thing I remembered was the pain against the back of my head as I fell to the floor.

Chapter Seven: The Blackness

HALLUCINATIONS. Step one, I thought through my slumber. With a gasp, I woke up to the coldness of the floor against my back, and I searched around the room. The bottom of the sink was all I could see. I didn't move because my head was thumping hard. Then it all came rushing back. I didn't really know what I had seen or what I thought I'd seen. I slowly lifted myself from the ground and used what little strength I had to push my body up. I curled my legs to stand. With each breath, I tried pulling myself to my feet, but I felt too uneasy. It felt like I was spinning. After I gave up trying to stand, I reached for the towel and wrapped it tightly around myself. I crawled slowly to the edge of the bathroom leading into the main room. I peered in the bedroom and saw that Jared still wasn't back. I pressed my hand against the back of my head to check for blood. Thankfully, all I felt was a bump forming.

I finally got the strength to stand and walked to the window, but I didn't see Jared. To my surprise, the car was still parked, and the sky was still dark. The stitches in my head were itchy and tight as I bandaged it back up.

Finding the remote on the edge of the bed, I clicked the television on and sat. "Dr. Alec Ravana is a revolutionary figure. He has found the cure to the Black Sickness, and we can't be more grateful to him. My son,

Ronnie, was dying just yesterday, and today he is able to speak again. We owe all our lives to him, and I think he knows how much his cure means to us."

I heard a click as the door opened. I jumped off the bed and ran to the corner, but was relieved to see it was just Jared. He stopped in the doorway and stared at me.

"I just needed time to think. I didn't leave. I walked the parking lot and then I was sitting outside the door." He hesitated as he came closer, and I saw he was holding bits of cloth. "I bear clothes." He put down a pair of jeans and a white long-sleeve shirt with red vans.

I looked in amazement. "Where did you find these?" I started to ask, but he laughed.

"I stole this from the lost and found. It was downstairs, and I'm sure that it is clean, but if you're scared to wear it, I can drive to the Laundromat."

"No, that's okay. Thank you for the clothes," I said indifferently.

He looked uncomfortable, looking me up and down while I stood in a towel. I was relieved that I was completely covered, but I couldn't help but feel the air in the room shift. I grabbed the clothes off the bed and then walked slowly back to the bathroom. I shut the door hastily behind me. I felt relieved for the moment, alone again. I changed into the clothes and was psyched. They fit perfectly, although the shoes were a little big. I put my old pair of socks on from my boots with money still stuffed in them and was pleased to find out that they fit closer to my size.

I walked back out into the room and found Jared sitting on the bed. He gave me a sweeping glance before looking down at his hands.

"There's something I want to talk about." He seemed nervous. "I want to tell you one thing before we go on." He hesitated and sat on the edge of bed. I sat to the side, tucking my legs beneath me, so I could face him. "People are after me, too. I should have told you, but they're after me because I won't join them."

"Join them in what?" I asked.

"In controlling the world," he said in all seriousness, but I couldn't help myself. I began to giggle because of the absurdity, but stopped quickly when his face turned sinister. "I'm being serious. They are trying to control the world, and they will succeed. They have already won. They've won because I don't know how to stop them."

I looked into his eyes and saw that he was telling the truth. He didn't even flinch away from my face like most do when they were lying. "How do you know they're going to try to control the world? And who is even trying to do this?"

"Dr. Ravana is trying to control the world, and I know this from your father." He stared at me intently.

"Dr. Ravana? But he is trying to help people." He worked with my father, and my father wasn't bad.

"Lena, you can't trust everyone you met." He seemed to regret the way he put it, because he hesitated, but he continued. "Do you really think this cure is good? It was untested and was just 'discovered' through Joseph. Seems a little weird, right?" he told me, and I nodded. I had to agree, but my father didn't make this cure for bad.

"Did my father make this cure? My father worked with Dr. Ravana, right?" I asked curiously, bracing myself onto the comforter for the right answer.

"I don't know." He looked away quickly.

"Well, how will we stop him?" I asked confidently, but he gazed at me as if I was a silly child, which was true. I was a ridiculously bashful girl, who was afraid to venture out into the world, at least in his eyes.

"Lena, we won't stop him until we find out what he is doing. And you won't be doing anything but staying out of sight. Do you understand?"

"I want to help. So how can I help? You can't stop me."

"Obviously, you can't be stopped. You climb and scale windows instead," he said laughing. He smacked my leg. I smiled with him, but quickly recovered by getting up slowly. His hand fell to his side. I tried to walk away, but he grabbed my arm. I winced, but he didn't seem to notice. "You can't help unless you know what everyone is dying to know."

"And what is that? I can rack my brain for it," I retorted coarsely.

"The true cure." I took a deep breath, but he continued. "We are going to my safe house. When we get there, we are going to research and find out what is going on."

I sat silently for a while, and he let me take my time. I was grateful for that.

"About this safe house, did you know this was coming?"

"Your dad told me so yes, I knew."

"Then why didn't you warn anyone?" I asked judgmentally.

He didn't answer, but instead he looked at me in surprise. "Why didn't you?"

I froze in place. "What are you talking about?"

"Your father was the leading man of research. Don't you remember anything?"

"If you'd talk to me, maybe I would be able to remember things," I said softly. "First off, my father was never around me. He was too busy finding the cure for cancer to tell me anything." He smiled at me, and I found myself smiling back.

"What?" I asked and felt my cheeks turning red.

"You just sound like any typical teenager girl who hated her parents."

"I didn't hate them. I loved them," I said defensively.

"I know that," he said softly.

A yawn escaped my lips before I could stop it. I tried to hide it with my hand, but Jared chuckled to my surprise.

"Okay, I guess we should get some rest." He began to move off the bed, but I grabbed hold of his shirt before I could stop myself. I jerked my hand away, but he stared at me, clearly confused because he mouth hung open in surprise. "Sorry, "I muttered. "It's just I don't want to sleep alone tonight."

What scared me was how true it was whenever I said it. "Stay on your side, and I'll stay on mine. I'd feel better knowing you're beside me and that you're not killing your back on the floor." I hesitated, thinking I had crossed some line, but he just nodded.

"Thank god. I wouldn't have gotten much sleep down there."

He didn't put up much of a fight. He threw himself into the bed as he got under the covers and sprawled out.

"Will you tell me about my father?" I asked softly in the night.

He was silent for a long time. I turned to face him and saw him gaping up at the ceiling. He cleared his throat, and I held my breath as he spoke. "Your father really loved you. He mentioned you all the time."

"What did you and he do all the time?"

"Mainly we discussed ways to save the world." He was silent, and I waited for more.

"Jared?" I asked silently, but I was met with soft snores. I smiled slightly and reached over to pull the cover more over his chest. I admired his face. The only light coming in was from the moon. I rolled over to face the wall, because I couldn't continue to stare at Jared. I felt safe beside him and I smiled. I closed my eyes and slipped into a deep slumber.

***

The cold wind pushed against my face, and my eyes burned. In the distance, I saw two figures walking toward me. I looked down and heard the delicate crunch underneath my feet. I had always loved the snow, even as I got older. Some people grew out of their love for the cold, wet weather, but I never would.

Two pairs of feet stopped me in my tracks; I looked up and saw that one of them was attractive. He held the girl he was with protectively against his shoulder. I couldn't see her face, but I knew that she must be hurt. I tried to speak to them, to ask what was wrong with the girl, but no words came out.

The girl seemed to be whispering to him, and he held her hand. Then the girl looked me right in the eyes. She had a hazel eye and a cloudy gray eye, but that wasn't what set her apart. It was the blackness all around her face. She pointed to my eye and then to hers. I didn't understand why.

A smell of burning skin and blood filled my nose. I tried to cover my nose, but my arms wouldn't move. She was rotting, and the smell was so strong I began to puke. The girl looked at me and held her arm out. The boy let her walk forward, and she pulled my hair up.

"There, there. It goes away. You get used to the feeling of death soon."

She punched me in the center of my belly, and I looked down. She had punched a hole through my stomach and I began to scream as she and the boy laughed insanely.

I heard the most curdling scream, and I lunged forward onto the bed. I searched around and saw that I was alone. The scream was my own. My stomach began to turn, and I ran to the bathroom, but the door was closed. I ran to the trashcan beside the bed and threw up as I did in my dream.

I tried to do so quietly so that Jared wouldn't come out. I had to throw the trash bag away in the hotel Dumpster, so Jared wouldn't find an unpleasant surprise.

I gathered the trashcan bag and almost dropped it. In the bag, there was only blood. I looked in the mirror and opened my mouth as I examined inside. No blood at all. I searched down in the trash, expecting it to disappear like it had before in the bathroom, but it didn't. I slumped down against the bed for a second. *Phase two*, I thought internally. This couldn't be happening for real.

I took the key that Jared put on the dresser beside the bed and walked outside the hotel door. The sun was rising, and it was beautiful outside. The trees around me had bright colors, and I smelt the crisp air. Nature had no clue about the turmoil the world was in and the cycle of life just continued as if there weren't rotting people all around. I walked down the stairs to the trashcan. It smelled horrible. It reminded me of my dream. It felt so real to me. I closed the door sharply after throwing away the trash. The smell of the Dumpster caused my stomach to churn, and I began to feel sick again. I backed up and leaned down slowly against a car.

I peered down at my arm. My skin was turning pink all around a small bruise that was forming. My suspicions were true. I knew they were true already, but I didn't want to face it. Dermadecatis began with a small bruise. I didn't cry. I had to be strong. I had the Black Sickness, just as my mother. We never did anything that we weren't supposed to do. The doctors sent precautions out each week in the newspapers. I read them every week for the past year and a half. I never had physical contact with anyone, and I didn't go out. My body felt weak and my head felt strange.

I laid my head into my hands, and I closed my eyes. I was going to fight this. If not, I was going to save others from this. I was going to save them from the people setting out to destroy the human race. I got up and walked boldly to the hotel lobby where the only computer was. The lobby was dark blue inside and there didn't seem to be anyone at the desk. I didn't bother asking if I was allowed to use the computer. I simply walked behind the desk and sat at the stool where the employees sat yesterday. I checked all around me, and it appeared that nobody was there at all. It was odd, but I didn't think anything of it, because I knew I wouldn't search long.

I typed in Dermadecatis and millions of posts came up. They each were stories of those who had died from the disease. A few links from the past three days told the stories of those who had been saved by the cure. It seemed to be going well for everyone. Nothing told me how the sickness came about or how it was spread. It was completely unknown. Some theorized that God sent

Dermadecatis down to destroy the world like he had done with a great flood.

They said that Dr. Ravana defied what God was trying to destroy. I closed my eyes and remembered my father speaking to my mom and me about the first case of Dermadecatis.

"Lily and Lena, we are making a breakthrough. You just don't—"

My mother cut him off before he could finish. "Isaac will die."

"No, he will not," he said harshly back.

"Honey, what is the purpose of this?" She looked to him with sad eyes.

"I have discovered very much about this disease and its symptoms. First off, there are hallucinations. Isaac has told me this many times. Vomiting comes next. The third symptom is that lumpy, black skin. Of course this is where the rotting comes into place." He paused, and I felt my eyes widening.

"Dad, can this happen to anyone?" I asked with fear.

"Not if I can find a way to stop to the disease." He smiled, but I didn't feel like smiling back. I didn't want anyone else to hurt from this disease.

"Sebastian," my mother spoke to him, "maybe we could talk about this in private." She looked to me, and I frowned.

"Anything we say, we can say in front of Lena. She is a part of this world and my discoveries."

He walked to me and picked up my hands and gently pulled me to my feet. "Lena," he said and touched my shoulder. "I am working on a cure, and I want you to be responsible for it. You can do it."

My mother sighed audibly and walked out of the room while rolling her eyes. My father caught sight of it and turned back to me.

"I am working on it. I am going to cure Isaac, and if I can't, I will cure the next case. When I die, you will be responsible for it."

I swallowed and nodded. *He kissed my cheek and followed where my mother had just left the room.*

I stared blankly at the screen. What made me so upset about the memory was that my father never found a treatment. Instead, I was left confused. He told me the antidote would be left to me, and yet, Dr. Ravana had the cure. My father never mentioned to me again about the remedy and there never was a cure made by him.

I wanted to distract myself from my thoughts so I decided to look up the cure. I found that many people were having some complications with it.

The cure had side effects such as black outs as well. There had been a recent story from someone with it. It said that he woke up from a black out, completely unsure what he had done, but he found himself in his home, in bed.

Whenever the Black Sickness attacked, it took your skin with it. This was the most sickening thing to happen, but it reminded you that your time was short. I didn't want to face the truth, but I had the Black Sickness. There was no denying it. I would save the world as my father asked me many years ago. I had to tell Jared. I had to believe these simple words—I was not weak. I was brave.

Chapter Eight: The Bleed Out

I DELETED THE history and logged off. I pulled the sleeves of my white shirt completely over my bruising skin, or rotting skin, I wasn't sure which, and walked swiftly back to the room. Hopefully, he didn't notice I had been gone.

I braced myself as I walked in the door, but to my relief, Jared was still in the bathroom. I closed the door slowly behind me and then turned on the TV. I didn't want to think about the disease, but of course, it was on the news.

"This just in, a new outbreak has overtaken a small town near Winston Salem. 3,006 lives have succumbed to Dermadecatis, and nearly 7 thousand more have shown signs and symptoms of the disease. Dr. Ravana is onsite working diligently to clean up." The screen switched over to Dr. Ravana bent over, working on a patient in the street.

I quickly turned off the TV in disgust and sat on the bed. The door opened to the bathroom. Jared walked out wrapped in a towel. He looked startled to see me awake.

"Hey. Did you go outside or something? Your cheeks are flushed."

I didn't say much. I just nodded. He returned to the bathroom, leaving the door open. "Don't go out in the open without me if you can help it," he said quickly. "Are you hungry? We need to hit the road, and we could go eat before we check out. Is that okay with you?"

"Yes, that's fine," I said, hoping my voice didn't falter.

I sat in silence as he got dressed in the bathroom. He appeared to have taken some clothes, too. While he looked severe in his leather jacket, I found that he looked softer in everyday clothes. He wore a gray long-sleeved shirt with jeans. He kept his signature combat boots.

We walked in silence out of the room and into the parking lot. He turned to me and asked if I was okay. I didn't answer him, because I didn't think I could lie. He left it alone, but his gaze lingered and he gave me a suspicious look by raising his eyebrows.

We crossed the parking lot and entered the tiny diner for breakfast. The place was dead, except for a few people. A couple with a dog sat at the counter along with a few lone men. I picked a booth by the window and sat. I gazed outside and immersed myself in the beauty, because I didn't know how long I would be able to enjoy the simple things. Dark clouds filled the sky. I loved the rain, because it always made me feel that we were going to get a fresh start to the next day. I didn't know how many new days I would have if I were sick.

The waitress came over to our table. If it weren't for the blonde hair, I would have thought Kaley had just walked up. Kaley had dark red hair and walked with a confidence that many confused with conceitedness. I missed Kaley, and I really hoped she was okay. I wished I had my cellphone to tell her I was doing fine. The waitress wasn't particularly friendly, but neither was I at the moment. She didn't look at me because she was admiring Jared. Which wasn't surprising. I couldn't help but feel annoyed when she bent over more than necessary to put down our menus. Yes, definitely like Kaley.

The waitress came back after a few moments of silence with Jared. I ordered pancakes and Jared ordered a mushroom omelet. While we waited, I tried to feel better by asking Jared questions.

I could tell he was expecting a silent breakfast, because when I spoke up he looked strangely at me. "Well, did you ever play any sports?"

He hesitated. "Uh, I played football until I was eleven and then I played baseball until I was fourteen. I gave up after because things came up."

"Like what?"

"My father and I didn't agree, so I quit to piss him off," he said with a smirk before turning to the window. "What about you?"

"Well, I never tried to make my dad unhappy, or my mom." He looked crossly at me. "I danced until I was a senior in high school." I felt sad inside as I remembered the last time I saw my parents. I quickly changed the subject. "Why don't you ask me a question now?"

"Hmm, that would require me to care."

"Hmph," I said with a smile. His face fell, and I wondered why. He was the one who wanted to end the conversation, and I was kidding. Our food arrived, ending the awkward moment. While I turned my attention to my pancakes, he brought up a subject I couldn't avoid.

"What's your favorite book? Or do you know how to read?" he asked while I poured the syrup over my pancakes.

"My favorite is *Looking For Alaska*." I read more than I could talk. "What about you? Or can you read anything other than television captions."

"Ouch. My favorite book is *Fight Club*. It's a movie with Brad Pitt, if you didn't know."

"And Edward Norton. You can't forget him." He nodded in approval.

He reached across the table "Let me try your coffee." He rudely grabbed my cup and took a huge gulp. I looked on in disgust. I felt a flutter of butterflies by how comfortable he was to drink after me.

"That doesn't taste as good as I thought." He placed it back in front of me, and I looked at him, testing his sincerity, waiting for it to falter.

"I don't want it now. Haven't you heard that the disease could spread through sharing drinks?" I sounded like my mother, but I didn't care. Sadness swept over me as I remembered that I was just like her. Too safe, leading to sickness anyway.

He chuckled darkly and leaned all the way over the table, and as I pushed back he whispered, "Then I would have it from kissing." He winked at me, and I grimaced. I didn't want to think of him kissing someone else. Then I stopped myself. Why should I care? He sat back again, watching me, and I crossed my arms.

He held my gaze for longer than necessary and I felt the blood rush to my face as I held my breath. I took a bite of my pancakes to break the stare, then I froze as I felt the acid coming up. I covered my mouth with my hand and dashed for the bathroom. I barely made it there before I threw up for the second time. *Crap, I wanted to tell Jared in a much better way than this.*

I flushed the blood down and went to the sink to wash my hands. I looked in the mirror and saw a few changes to my face. My skin color had gone to a ghastly white color and my lips were chapped and bright red. I looked down to my arm and saw there were black splotches or bruises along it.

My forehead was covered with the white cloth. I felt so different, and the room started to spin. There was a soft knock on the ladies room, and I knew it was probably Jared waiting for me. I opened the bathroom door and Jared stayed outside.

"Hey, I paid the bill. I bet you're catching a bug." Thank god, I didn't have to tell him this way. "Let's go check out of the hotel, and we'll be on our way. Do you think you'll be up for a car ride?"

"I think I can handle it. We can take a bucket," I said weakly and let out a steadied laugh.

"I hope I don't get sick or get your weird ways. Just kidding." I didn't retort back. He noticed because he stopped me. Looking me right in the eyes, he asked, "Is everything okay?"

I walked past him and said loud enough for him to hear, "I like you better when you're sullen. Suits you better." I knew he stopped in place, because I didn't hear his footsteps any longer. He finally regained himself and passed me without a glance as he led the way.

As we walked to the hotel, I noticed that it was mildly dead around the whole parking lot. I was sure most people had checked out so we walked to the front desk, where I was looking up the cure earlier.

As we walked up, a smell hit us square on. It smelled like venom to my nose. Not again! It was the smell from my dream. We froze in place as the smell of blood captivated our senses. I would know the scent anywhere. I remembered it very clearly from the day my parents died.

Jared and I both stopped dead in our tracks. We stared at each other for the first time since our tiny spat.

Jared walked to the desk and laid the key down on the table. He hesitated as if he had discovered something and waved me back as I tried to approach him. Which only made me to want to move closer.

As I did, the smell grew stronger, and he gave me a reproaching look. Jared stepped behind the desk, and he opened the door behind it. He shut the door fast, but I moved closer and opened it myself, as he stood stunned.

On the ground, the woman who checked us in laid with blood spilling from her head. Her husband was next to her, facing the ground. As I began to scream, I felt a rough hand clasp over my mouth.

My instincts took over, and I bit down hard. I felt my teeth quiver from the hardness and coldness of the hand. It didn't feel right; it felt like I bit down on glass. The bite didn't do much because it didn't even move, and I heard no gasp. I jammed my elbow back as hard as I could, hitting him on his chin. Nothing happened again, but I felt a stab of pain from the contact. The hand released me. I turned around to see that Jared hit him with something that looked like an ashtray bowl. In that moment, I did the only thing that I knew could hurt any man. I kneed him right where it hurt, and he threw himself onto the floor.

I looked down with victory and saw it was Joseph. He found us. I took off running and was surprised to see he wasn't coming after us. Jared and I reached the car, and I threw myself into the seat as it revved to life. We got onto the highway before my heart began to slow. He began to laugh. I looked at him in disbelief.

"What's so funny? We could have died. He killed an innocent man and woman for what reason?" This only made him laugh even harder, and I could only think of how morbid he was to think that someone dead was funny.

"Lena, you kicked him." He laughed so hard he looked aspirated. "I underestimated you. You go for the low blows," he barely let out. He cackled hard, and I couldn't help but join in.

"My dad taught me self-defense, or a little. The first two things didn't work so I tried the one thing that I knew would," I said with a genuine smile. I missed my father, and I was glad something he left with me paid off.

"Well, it worked. How do you feel now that you successfully took care of your self?" He smirked, but I answered seriously.

"I feel okay," I said with a little uncertainly. "Why did he kill them? They were just in the wrong place at the wrong time, and why was he alone this time?"

He looked gloomy. "These people are not what you think. They don't play games. They will kill whatever is in the way, and they will kill us if we don't get to our safe house. You will be safe and you are going to survive." He hesitated. "As for being alone. I have no idea why he was sent alone."

I didn't answer because I knew he tried to keep me safe, but he just couldn't save me from this. I would never be better, and I would die. But I felt calmer knowing that he would be in the safe house. I would risk anything to keep him safe, because I wasn't anymore. I understood now that he was simply trying to protect me and everyone else from the horrors of the world. He had risked his life one time too many, and I owed him. I was going to save the world, and it started with keeping Jared out of harm's way.

"Yeah, you will be safe, too," I said because that was the only thing I could guarantee.

Chapter Nine: A Monster

WE DROVE FOR forty minutes before Jared cursed because we had to stop for gas. He must've forgotten that we would have to take a rest. We got off the exit toward an Exxon gas station. "If we would have had jet packs, we would have been to the safe house in three hours," he scoffed. "Three hours." *Jetpacks? How silly,* I thought while shaking my head.

As we pulled into the lot, I asked if he would walk inside so I could go to the restroom. He told me that he would. I felt afraid to go in, but I didn't want us to be separated. Whenever something came after us, I wanted them to know I would do everything to protect Jared and not myself.

Jared got out and followed me. He walked behind me as if he wanted to protect me. I wanted to tell him there wasn't a point; I'd probably be dead from the disease soon, anyway.

We entered the gas station, and I asked a stubbly man behind the counter where the bathroom was. He only threw a hand up to the left of the store. Jared stayed behind and searched through the gas station for food. "Want anything?"

"I want some Twizzlers," I said with a smile.

"On it," he said, searching down the aisle.

I walked down a dimly lit, narrow hallway. The walls were a flaxen color and the floor was bright red. I had to wait for someone in the bathroom. I listened to the music and closed my eyes as I waited. I hummed along to the melody and smiled as the song progressed. The door opened abruptly and a girl almost five feet tall came out with short blonde hair. She didn't look at me but into the distance. I couldn't even see what she looked like as she walked away. I felt uneasy as she descended the hallway, but I shook my head to snap out of it.

I entered the bathroom and found my reflection in the mirror. I looked a mess. I wondered if I should try to look decent now. Then again, Jared already knew that I was a disaster. I moved my sleeve up, and I was appalled at how much it had changed.

The black specks from that morning had turned to deep red and black blotches all over my arm. It looked as if it had been bleeding for a while, but there was no blood on my white shirt. The cut seemed to be healing, and it didn't look bad. It was the surrounding area that wasn't okay. I felt like crying, but I moved the fabric back over my skin. Out of sight, out of mind, as people used to say. That was bullshit. I choked back tears and looked straight in the mirror. I told myself to stop being a coward. Maybe I should just tell Jared. He could take me to get the cure. That was what I had to do. I had to march out there and tell him that this was what had to be done. I would tell him, but I would be strong, no matter what.

I jerked the door open with force and confidence, but stopped short. The girl with the pixie cut blonde hair was standing directly in front of it. Her face was right against it, and she smiled in a sinister way.

"Is everything okay?" I asked. Then she turned her head to the side and quickly reached for my arm. I jerked back. I began to slam the door in her face, but she stopped it with her foot. She kicked it open hard and I fell to the ground against the filthy sink. She smiled as she looked at me with her bright blue eyes. Her stare was so fierce I almost felt as if my body was going to burst into flames just from a stare.

"Ah, you must be Lena," she said, and as she did she took my arm and turned it until I screamed. "Hmm, looks like you're sick. Maybe I should take you with me."

She laughed as I screamed, and I looked into her eyes again. This time they weren't blue but flashed into an emerald color, just like Max's once had. She began talking so fast I could barely catch on to her words, all I could hear was, "here....come...."

She was talking into her arm. I was taken aback at the scene before me. Although she looked ridiculous, she was going to take me, or worse than that, kill me. She must have been calling for those who wanted Jared and me dead, so I acted fast. I bit down onto the hand that was holding me, and I kicked her as hard as I could in the stomach. She let go, which surprised me, and I got up hastily. I ran as fast as my legs let me, which wasn't very impressive. Jared was standing at the counter when I ran to him and he looked to me as if I were crazy.

"What's wrong?" he yelled to me.

"Run!" I managed to scream at the top of my lungs. I felt winded, which must have been a side effect of the sickness. As I yelled this, I felt someone hit the back of my head hard, and I yelped as I fell to the ground. I watched as the man behind the counter suddenly jumped onto Jared. As Jared tumbled down, I felt another pound against my skull.

The corners of my eyes were blurry, and I saw black blotches around me. I closed my eyes and laid my head against the tile floor. As soon as I did, the banging instantly stopped, and the weight of the girl seemed to have been lifted off me. I slowly opened my eyes and saw the man who jumped on Jared was against the wall, with the girl beside him. Jared had one hand curled around each of their necks and they were being lifted from the floor. I didn't know how he had the strength to do this or how Jared got both of them with ease, but I did know I was useless in protecting him. He didn't need me; he could protect himself and me.

"Who sent you here?" he screamed at the girl in a far too scary tone.

I slowly got up as he let go of her neck to slam his fist into her nose. Normally, I would oppose this behavior, but right now it seemed appropriate. He grabbed her neck again while rising her off the floor.

"No one sent me. I'm here because if I find her," she shot her deadly glance at me, "I get a bonus. And if I get you, I get the cake," she struggled out.

"Why do they want her? Do you know?" he demanded, but she didn't answer. Jared tightened his grip on her neck, and she let out a strangled sound before he loosened back up.

"No, I don't know. We aren't allowed to ask questions. I don't even know who sends me the messages. But I'm after her, and I'm not leaving without her. She's going to die anyway." She laughed an evil little laugh, and I cringed at the sound.

"She won't die. I will protect her. I've done a good job of it already."

"We won't kill her, but that disease will. Hasn't she told you?" She laughed insanely at the stare he must have been giving her. My heart was sinking. I should have already told him, but I was too afraid.

I didn't see his face, but I felt the atmosphere change as he slowly turned his gaze over to my eyes. I dropped mine to the floor quickly, and he knew that it was true. I peered back up and was surprised he didn't scream because his face looked like it was in outrage. He turned back to the girl who was still smiling at me.

"We are leaving, and you will stay here. You, too." He pointed to the man who hadn't said a word.

"Don't worry. We won't move," the man said. "They're almost here. They'll catch you." The man looked over to the girl and they smiled as their eyes flickered to emerald like flames.

Jared didn't have to tell me twice to run. He grabbed my good arm, and we darted for the car. As we got into it, the sky turned from light to dark in a matter of seconds. I peered up, and it looked as if five hundred birds were in the sky. Jared started the ignition and then drove full throttle. We reached the end of the street when about forty figures dropped from the sky in front of us. They all had emerald eyes.

My screams filled the air.

"Calm down," Jared shouted back to me. The sky was so dark it seemed as if it were 12:00 at night rather than 3:00 in the afternoon.

"Drive!" I shouted through the darkness.

"It won't do us any good, Lena. They won't move."

They all walked forward steadily. He pulled out his gun that had moved Max and Joseph out of the way two days ago, and many moved now, but a few of them continued to walk forward with ease.

Jared began to drive in reverse, but more waited for us there. I shut my eyes and covered my ears because they all spoke in sinister voices. All of them were chanting my name. I started to scream. This was the end. I could feel it.

As I screamed, the chanting grew louder and I started screaming louder. "Shut up! Shut up," I said silently while bending over in my seat.

The chanting surrounded me now as I yelled into the air. I held my necklace tightly in my hands as tears built in my eyes, and I cried, "Go away." The chanting stopped, and I stared up. I caught a glimpse of the last few people, flying up into the air. I froze. They had all left.

Jared looked over to me and it was as if he was frozen over as well. "What did you just do?" He looked to me curiously.

"Uh. Me?" I looked around and the sky was clear once more. "They're probably coming back. I didn't do a thing."

He began to drive again, and we turned onto the highway. "I wonder how safe we are. Maybe they're tricking us. I don't think we'll be safe for long. Why do they keep letting us go? This is ridiculous. I don't understand. Are they just trying to scare us?" he stammered out. And I sat in silence. Did they leave because of me?

Jared let the conversation go, but now I feared he thought I was a coward for not telling him I was sick. He looked confused and he seemed to be frantically racking his brain for an explanation to what just happened. Maybe he would forget that I didn't tell him that I was sick.

"Lena. I want to talk about something." He was thinking about it. "Will you just tell me if she was being serious?"

I didn't answer, and he stopped the car. Just as he did, the storm I saw in the clouds at the diner finally caught up to us. The rain pattered on the vehicle, and I looked out the window toward the dark rainclouds. "Uh, Jared. This doesn't seem safe. We need to keep going."

"Show me where it is." I sat in place, not looking at him but instead at the ground. He raised his voice, "Show me it. Now!" he screamed into the darkness of the car.

I stared at him in shock and pulled my sleeve up obediently and watched his face. It turned to anger, disbelief, hurt and pain in all of three seconds. He turned the car back on and continued to drive. He didn't speak.

"Jared," I said calmly, but he didn't respond. "Can we talk about this?"

He looked into the distance on the road. "Lena. I understand why you didn't tell me. I'm nothing to you. But I would have at least liked to know about this. I could have taken more precautions. How did you even?" He stopped talking, and I watched him take a deep breath and sigh. "When did it show up?" he shouted more to himself than me.

"The hotel," I said. He shook his head in bewilderment, but he didn't have any answers about the disease as I had hoped. We rode for about thirty minutes as I waited for him to talk. I refused to speak so I started a countdown in my mind. If he didn't talk in ten minutes, I would just lay it out there.

Right before I was about to speak, he said, "Why didn't you tell me? I could have helped you. What if I could have stopped it?"

I stared blankly outside. "What could you have done? There is nothing to be done. It's here and I'll die. Maybe I should go get the cure."

He slammed his hand onto the dashboard and screeched, "You will not get the cure, Lena. I won't allow that at all!"

"Why not?" I shouted back to him. "You think you can control me? I'm dying. Why do you want me to die, Jared? So you don't have to deal with me or protect me?" The anger built up in me until I was shaking.

He stopped the car for the second time. "What good are you dead?"

"What does that even mean? You keep saying that, but I'm not good to you alive either." It stung to know that I would die without a purpose. Without helping anyone at all.

He acted as if I never spoke at all. "Lena, I have been observing those with the cure while you slept at the hotel. I've tried to understand what the catch is. And I think I've figured it out. The cure is mind control. I don't know how and I don't know what the cure is, but it isn't safe. I won't lose you that way. I won't let you get the cure until I know what it is. You saw them. You saw Joseph," He yelled.

He was right. Their eyes were strange. The other thing was the fact that these people were super human.

"Were those." I hesitated. "What are those things? Those people. Are they even people?"

"Those things back there had the cure, I'm almost positive. I don't know what they are, but I'm sure Gabe will have answers. We'll have to contact him. Maybe he can find a cure for you. The world needs you," he told me. I was lost because why would the world need me?

The sick girl with the disease? I had to try to save them even if I didn't know how.

"I want to save them," I said silently.

"Then we will. Together," he said as he reached his hand over to me and squeezed.

***

We approached an abandoned shopping mall, and Jared pulled to the back. He reached for the bulky phone and told me he would be right back. I rolled down the window to listen, but he was all the way down the sidewalk along the woods. I caught a glimpse of my head in the side mirror and gulped.

My forehead had gotten a dark spot around it, and I knew what it meant. It was spreading. I almost retched as I caught sight of my arm with pieces of dark colored skin flaking off. I started to bleed a little, and the smell was excruciating. The smell coming from my arm could only be described as death. There was barely any undamaged tissue and it was spreading fast. The blackness was rising up my arm toward my shoulder, but it wasn't quite there yet. I fought back the tears burning my eyes. Crying wouldn't fix anything. I had to be strong. I had to be strong for everyone.

Jared climbed back into the car and turned to me.

"Gabe said he's put a watch on the car and he'll keep track of the people chasing us."

"How can he do that? My dad's car doesn't have a tracking chip in it," I told him in an unbelieving tone.

He smiled at the sound of astonishment in my voice. "Gabe can do anything. Seriously. He'll signal us if we are being chased."

"How are we going to see the signal?"

He laughed, and said, "Oh. We'll know." He started the car and drove onto the main road again.

"Since you refuse to answer anything I ask, how about this?" I said annoyed. "How long until we make it?"

"I'm going to speed up. This car is capable of going faster than the speed limit."

"That didn't answer my question," I said frustrated, but he ignored me. "What if a cop catches you speeding?"

"Well, they would have to catch us first." And then I lurched forward.

Chapter Ten: The Drive

WE GOT INTO North Carolina fast. I looked to the speedometer and realized that Jared had been driving about 160 the whole way. He weaved in and out of the cars on the highway. I was very happy to see that there even were people out. At least the entire United States wasn't like Texas. I began sweating because I was scared, or maybe it was another side effect of the disease. My father never mentioned that, though.

I didn't know why the cops hadn't stopped us or tried to, but then, I didn't remember seeing any along any of the roads. Maybe they weren't something we needed anymore because the death rate continued to climb. I looked over to Jared. He hadn't spoken to me for almost an hour. I hadn't noticed how tightly he was gripping the steering wheel.

"What's wrong?" I asked him as I glanced out the window to the woods speeding by along the highway.

"Lena, I didn't want to tell you what Gabe and Holland found out." He tensed up even more, and I saw the vein in his forehead. I wanted to tell him to calm down, that everything would turn out all right, but I didn't believe it myself.

"What are you talking about?" I asked collectedly.

"The cure. On the phone, Gabe told me that he has been researching. He found someone lingering outside the safe house. They were trying to find a way in so Gabe actually took him inside because he suspected he had the cure. He did. And Gabe tried to look inside him to see what the cure actually is." He shut his eyes for a half a second. "Just a small incision."

"What did he find?" He didn't speak. I felt my forehead getting clammy as I panicked. "Jared! Talk to me."

He took a deep breath before answering. "Gabe said he didn't find anything because when there was an incision made, the person exploded." He stopped speaking, and I felt my eyes water. An innocent person died. "Gabe's upset. He thinks they are set for self-destruction if they are tampered with. It's completely ludicrous, and Gabe is really torn up about it." Jared let me sit in silence for a second.

"Well, what does that mean for the others? There is no way to get them back to who they were?" I asked through the silence.

Jared spoke serenely but frustrated. "That won't happen to you because you won't have the cure."

"I don't care about me! I don't want these people to die," I told Jared. I didn't want anyone else to die. It wasn't fair. "What can we do?"

"Gabe has told us to come as soon as possible because you could die without the cure now. Lena, someone is messing with you specifically because you have all the answers."

"I have no answers at all!" I howled. "I have absolutely nothing to give them."

"Calm down. Jeez," he scoffed. "Listen, the disease was manmade. Someone made this disease so they could give you and the others the cure." I was silent and I felt my body tense. I felt my heart beating in my chest. Thankfully, he didn't notice my tensed body now. "They want to control your mind, so they can get answers.

They want to know what your father knew and created. They want full control of the world."

I let this sink in and sat in silence. I was unsure what to do or say.

"We'll figure this out, and you have to have patience with me. We have to be a team and not fight over this. When we get to Gabe, we'll have more answers about the disease," he reassured me.

"How do you know so much?"

"I know everything I know from your father. I've have told you this already. Why don't you believe me?" He balked, frustrated.

"I just wonder why he never told me. He never mentioned your name or any warnings about the disease or the fact that I'm so crucial to the world." I was lying, but I wanted to know more from Jared first. "I just don't know who to trust sometimes. Sometimes I ask him to send me a sign, and he never does." I felt hurt, but I didn't let him know it. "It's silly, but my dreams always give me answers. That's my only source of a sign," I told Jared.

"He probably does send signs. You just don't pay attention to them. He was a smart man. He'll find a way to get to you. Dreams are real, too, Lena."

I let that sink in. Maybe I needed to look at my dreams differently. He always wanted to confuse me. I bet my dad just didn't want me to have things to come to me so easily. He wanted me to work for everything, but I really needed to know if I should trust Jared. I didn't know if he was tricking me or using me to get to the information.

"I will not let this disease kill you. For your dad and myself and the world."

"For you?" My heart began to flutter. Was it true, after being together for a few days, that he was feeling something, too?

"Yes, I care for you. I know more about you than you think."

"What is that supposed to mean?" I asked silently.

"I never stopped checking on you after I left."

I regarded him questionably. "How did you check on me? I never left my house after my family died," I said calmly but a little frightened.

"Well, I checked because it was my orders. But I didn't watch you. I'm not a creep." He chuckled under his breath. "I watched the house, not you. I didn't invade your privacy. I listened around the town. Your little friend, Kaley, liked to talk about you all day long."

I looked over in shock. I felt hurt. I knew I had no friends, but I thought Kaley was at least my friend when my family died. "What did she say about me?" He couldn't be telling the truth. Not about Kaley.

"She just said how you never left the house. I don't want to talk about it. Just know she isn't your friend, and she would've turned on you if you had stayed any longer."

I felt discomfort fall over me. She was my friend. I was sure of it. Kaley had stuck with me through everything. "That's a mistake. She wouldn't do that," I told him a little questioningly.

"She talked about me a lot. She said I hurt you, and you deserved it. She told others that you needed everyone to like you, and when one person didn't, you went insane. Then you locked yourself up in the house."

"I literally think no one likes me. And for the record, I was in the house because my family died," I said bitterly. I couldn't believe it. That was something Kaley would say. She used the line many times about Katherine. She always told me that Katherine went insane when someone didn't like her. Anger flooded me. If I ever saw her again, I would probably punch her in the face. "I guess you feel the same way about me. You think I'm selfish," I said angrily. "And don't be so flattered. I didn't go insane."

"Look, I see who you are. I don't think you're selfish." I felt my face burning and knew that it was bright red. I was glad the night's sky blocked this from his view. "And I know you're not insane," he said softly.

"You're speeding way too much," I said to break the conversation as my cheeks flushed more intensely.

"Well, why don't you sleep?" he asked softly.

"I think I will." I shut my eyes and before I drifted to sleep, I felt a hand brush against my face.

***

As I walked home through the neighborhood I grew up in, the world around me seemed a blur. I felt the thick air everywhere, but I didn't fight it like I used to. When my mom was alive, she told me to cover my mouth if I felt the air wasn't right.

I remembered when my father would sit up all night in his office. As I walked home, I saw the doors wide open. My mother never left anything open on account of my father saying he wouldn't be able to work with the doors open.

So I took off running to get to the door. A gust of wind blew against my face as I reached it. I heard screaming coming from my mother and I fought against the wind to reach her. Why would my father leave my mom alone?

As I entered the front door, an unnerving silence surrounded me. I stopped in place because the normal room I was so accustomed to was no longer there. The room was black with red all around. There was something on the floor, but I couldn't tell what it was. As I neared it, I realized that it was my mother covered in blood, and she was reaching her hand out toward my dad's office. I knelt, but she was cold. It was odd that I didn't feel bad about her dying for a second time. I felt numb to the sight of her dead.

I continued down the hallway and neared the door to my father's office. It was wide open, and I walked in. He walked toward me and a dark omen was around him, but as he approached, a glow enveloped around him. He smiled at me and tilted his head as if to exam me. Just as he reached my forehead, a hand clasped over his mouth, and he hunched over.

"Daddy!" I tried to yell out, but little noise came out of my mouth.

He slowly rolled back up and faced me. He kissed my check and touched my forehead. A burning sensation ran through my body, and I began to scream as he smiled down at me.

"Don't be fooled by anyone, Lena. The key lies in you and you alone. I have figured out the truth and the truth lies in you as well. I know they have tried to kill you, but this is just the beginning. They have won until you can take their winnings. Don't let them continue to win. Let them help you get the disease out, but that's it. Do you understand?" He looked at me, and I nodded. "I don't have much time, but if you trust everyone you meet, you will be controlled. I cannot tell you all because I would mess with everything. I love you, Lena. This will work out, but if it doesn't work out for you, I will give Jared the knowledge."

I wanted to ask if Jared was really a part of this plan, or if my dad didn't tell Jared the plan. But I didn't get the chance to because he continued.

"Lena, he knows the plan to a degree. He is here to protect you from everyone. But you will ultimately save yourself and

others. Listen to your heart and what you hold dear. I will send you my love and guide you. This is where I leave you. I love you."

I woke up with a gasp, and I looked around. The car was completely empty. I began to frantically move around in search of Jared. I sighed when I saw he was outside the car, pacing back and forth. He looked to me from outside the car and grinned.

"Well, we're here. I think. I always get confused. Come on out." He opened the door for me and grabbed my hand to pull me up. My heart gave a leap from the contact. I stepped down onto the sand and smiled. This was like home. "I'm going to pull the car around. You stand here and wait. I'm parking it away from us, and I don't want you to have to walk too much. Stay right here and don't move. If danger comes, I will be here. I promise." And I believed him. He touched my face and left without another word.

I waited as he went to park, feeling shockingly calm and reassured. I was not sure where he went. I looked out to the ocean and sat in the sand. The breeze brushed my hair from my face, and I played with it in my hands. It was wet from the rain, but I didn't mind, because the scene before me was breathtaking. The moon shined brightly down onto the water where I could see it perfectly. I had good memories involving the beach.

In that moment, I didn't care how long it took him to come back. I was happy there in my own little world. I thought about the dream I just had. I was alone. I had to bear the entire world on my shoulders. How could I do it? How could I do what my father hadn't been able to? Why did my father leave the world in my control? I didn't want to have everyone's life to deal with when I couldn't even handle my own.

Jared walked back to me, and I didn't even jump when he tapped my shoulder. He told me we would have to get moving before the day broke. "Can we go on the beach soon?" I asked quietly.

"How about now? I don't think I can let you outside when we get in the safe house. We actually have to walk along the shore until we find the safe house." I smiled as I ran down to the water, and I was hit with a harsh truth. I didn't think I would walk out of the safe house as I walked in.

Chapter Eleven: The Safe House

I WALKED BEHIND as Jared sped up. He circled the sand around me and jogged beside me slowly. I thought of my dream and wondered if my father wanted me to trust Jared or not. I couldn't decide. The truth was, I did trust Jared. I felt something for him. I let the thought slip away. I couldn't decide if I made this dream up in my mind, so I didn't get close to anyone because I would be sick and die soon, or my dad came to visit me while I slept. I would like to choose the latter. We walked a while. Jared halted as we passed three lifeguard chairs.

"What is it?" He didn't answer, so I continued walking.

His voice broke through the crisp air. "Are you going to keep walking, or do you want to get into the safe house?" he asked in a strict voice.

I turned around amazed as I saw the lifeguard chair in the middle was laying flat on the ground, like an opening to a top. The sand had been moved to the side to reveal a breakage in the ground. Light was peering out of it, and I was in complete awe. I shouldn't have been so impressed by technology, because this was what my father showed me every day before. I loved it and envied those who were tech savvy.

"Wow." That was all I could manage to say as I looked to see if anyone was watching, but there appeared to be no one around.

"Ladies first," he said politely.

"All right," I said rudely and pointed to the hole in the sand. I stood there waiting for him to jump and he smirked.

"Honestly? You should probably go first. Just in case someone is out here waiting for you." I shivered, but I wouldn't budge. I didn't want to be out here, but I was unsure what awaited me down there.

"No one got me when I was alone," I retorted as his face turned sour. "What do I do to get in there?" I asked a little nervous.

"Just jump. Gabe has it set to whenever you jump a gust of air slows you down and you land on your feet." He shifted his weight to look at me more evenly.

"Is that possible?" I asked in astonishment.

"Anything is possible for Gabe. You'll soon find out." He beamed at me. "Just go ahead. Whenever you land. Move to the left and then don't budge or touch a thing. I have to deactivate everything." I didn't move, and he saw the doubt in my stare. "Trust me for once."

"What..." That was all I managed because his look silenced me.

"Okay." I stepped forward and looked once more at him and jumped. It reminded me of jumping into the pool. After that first step, you can't do anything but feel the water. You can't stop yourself. Sure enough, a gust of wind caught me as I slowly reached the floor. I laughed in awe as I glanced up the opening to see Jared peering down from very far up.

At the bottom, there was a long hallway to a doorway. I looked to the left and there was another hallway with about thirty computers lining the walls. In the center of the room, there was a large screen. I was amazed that so many machines could be in one small room.

I moved to the left as instructed just as Jared landed beside me. As soon as he did, an alarm sounded as the room turned pitch black. There was no way to see the computers, and I grabbed Jared's hand just as I had in the elevator. I pulled away in surprise and my heart began to beat in the darkness. There were voices and I didn't know what they were saying except, "trapped here forever." The lifeguard chair that was above us closed with a *thud* and we were surrounded by complete darkness.

Jared didn't seem to be afraid, but he started chuckling and said under his breath, "That's a new one." I was guessing he had been in this room before. I listened closely because the voices had stopped and had been taken over by vigorous typing.

"Access denied." A voice said out of nowhere. There was a blue light that shined into my eyes and then in a place across the room, which must have been Jared's brown eyes.

"Jared, no last name. There is one other person here. Access denied."

No last name? How curious could one person be? I didn't understand him and how he seemed to never have a full name. Maybe he was abandoned and wanted his real name changed. I was too afraid to point out that he didn't have a last name. I didn't understand how he made me feel, either. I knew I felt safe and protected whenever he was around. I had forgotten that feeling since my parents died.

There was even louder typing and once again the voice spoke. "Access denied. Unidentified person in the room has not been evaluated. Access denied."

I heard his voice from across the room. "I get it, but this is Lena Alona." There was a pause and the blue light flickered to me once more. I felt a prick on my finger and gasped in pain. I put it into my mouth and tasted blood. Then I felt a yank of my hair and realized that it was being pulled out.

Just then the lights flickered on and the computers shut down. "Access Granted."

The door slowly rose to a long narrow white hall, and Jared looked back at me, waving me forward. The only sound I heard was my heart pounding, and my feet wouldn't move me forward.

"Why is my name so important to everyone?" I saw that he wanted to laugh by the way he bit down his lip, but he didn't. My heart fluttered as I looked at him in the hallway light. He really was something. "Can I change my name?" I asked defiantly.

He let out a tight laugh. "Then we wouldn't have gotten in," he said through his laughter, and I frowned.

"Yeah, we wouldn't be in this mess either," I reminded him sadly.

He touched the small of my back as he guided me forward and didn't shove me like he normally did. My heart sped up from his touch, and I was immediately frustrated that he made me feel this way. We walked through the door, and it slammed down behind us. I looked back and there was only a wall there now. There was no way out. There wasn't a panel to get out. We were trapped.

"How do you leave?" I asked quietly.

"You don't," he said in a sinister voice. "Just kidding. Not this way. There's a different way to leave. Don't worry. If you want to live, you should have a little faith in me, and trust," he said in all seriousness.

"Why are you being nice to me right now?" I tested through the silence.

"Oh." He looked confused. "Would you rather me to be cruel to you?" I looked away. I shouldn't have said anything, but he lifted my chin to force me to look at him. "Well, I just want you to know that I'm not mean. I've just had a hard life. So have you, and I should have respected that before."

I didn't respond but stiffly nodded and pulled my face from his hands. I continued to walk, but he stayed behind for a second, and I heard a sigh. I didn't know why, but he made me feel so happy. I hated to feel this way when it might be too late for him to love me.

The hallway was white, but all along the walls there were beautiful paintings and tables with flowers on them. It looked like a home. We turned the corner, and I was in awe. This was an underground house. The room was open with a large couch and kitchen to the left. The couch was a cream color with brown trim around it. The walls were a warm brown. The kitchen had burgundy walls with flowers painted along the wallpaper. The house was filled with the scent of warm vanilla, and I couldn't help but wonder if Jared's mother lived there or if another woman lived in the house underground, just waiting for Jared.

The smell filled me up, and I felt happy and secure. It was unsettling, because I didn't know if it was too late for me to feel at home somewhere. I was determined to fight this disease with my mind as cancer patients fight their cancer.

"They must be down in the lab," Jared quietly told me.

"Wait. Who is waiting down there?" I asked all of the sudden feeling self-conscious. I touched my forehead and felt ridiculous. Of course they knew I was sick.

"Holland and Gabe," he exclaimed like I should have known the answer.

I followed him down the hall to another narrow hallway. This one was black and expanded to ten sets of doors. The door we approached was painted black and white. Jared opened it at the end of the hall and it led to a long corridor with stairs. They went down for what seemed like ages, and I was exposed to a brightly lit room. Inside the lab were twenty computers just like before and there was a long table for people to sit at. Along the table there was a long and wide television screen on the wall, but I didn't think it was used for entertainment. There was another large table on the other end of the room where many items sat.

In the center of the table, a boy bent over a machine with wires sticking out. A girl with strawberry-blonde hair that flowed all the way down her back sat beside the machine on the table. She looked bored and was staring longingly at her nails. She scowled whenever the boy made a sound. Neither of them glanced up. They seemed to be connected somehow, because she continued to clean the tools he used as he held them up. She would give him new ones as if he had told her he needed them, but they weren't even talking.

"Holland, you have to help. I can't do this alone; I have to activate the system. I think Jared will be here any minute," said the boy.

"Oh please, Jared will get past the system fast, don't you think?" Holland assumed quickly.

"I did." Jared spoke up. They both looked up with shocked faces. "You were supposed to be watching for us. You changed the system. Why?" he asked quietly, so quietly it sounded completely menacing.

The boy peeked up from behind the machine he was working on. He had dark curly hair and square glasses on his face. He was short and muscular, but his head looked as if it weighed the most on his body.

"Jared, we have to change the system every week. Come on, don't you remember?" He walked toward Jared while wiping his hands off on a towel. Holland sat in place with a dumbfounded look. I was starting to realize he sounded frustrated all the time. "We changed it when you left. We didn't exactly expect you back," he uttered, and I was struck by his comment. Why would he say that? Did he think we wouldn't make it there? "We knew you would get past it. I only remembered just now." Jared didn't respond so the boy continued, "Come help me? I'm trying to activate the transformer. Remember? We built this together, but now it's malfunctioning, so I tried to make it something new." He patted Jared on the back as if to say hello and completely bypassed me.

"New how?" Jared perked up. He seemed to have already forgotten that he was concerned about the system being changed.

"It is going to be small enough to transfer into a suit for us to wear. You know?" Gabe said while looking relieved because he distracted Jared.

"Look, let's work on it later. Holland, come over here." Jared realized the smugness on my face. He returned to his normal smile, but it didn't quite reach his eyes. "This is Lena, Gabe." Holland reached us as Gabe smiled deeply in my direction until he noticed my forehead. His gaze dropped, and he started pacing backward away from us. As Holland approached us,

Gabe walked away back to his project, to avoid me, I was sure. "Holland, this is Lena."

She smiled at me and didn't even look up at my forehead. She kept gazing into my eyes and that was it. "Hello, darling, it is so nice to meet you. You're so beautiful. Jared failed to mention that, or Gabe did. Who knows?" Jared walked over to Gabe, and it looked as though they were arguing. Holland must have sensed this too because she led me up the stairs into the house.

"I'm so glad to have another woman around. I love it here, but I miss people. Gabe is okay, but I just need a girl sometimes. Hey, want to see your room? I fixed it up myself. I hope you like purple. It's my favorite color. Well, pink is too, but I didn't know how you'd feel about pink." She rambled on as I peeked back downstairs. Gabe and Jared seemed to be in deep conversation. Gabe had wrinkled up his forehead, and Jared had his scary glance on Gabe.

I could barely get a word in until now so I just smiled and shook my head. "I love purple. Don't worry." I appreciated when someone spoke, because I didn't have to figure out what to say.

She smiled, and I could tell she felt accomplished and proud of her work. "I love the library, but I can let Jared show you. He built that for himself." I was shocked, because I didn't know that we had something in common like loving books. I laughed internally because he didn't show his love for books. Maybe he was afraid to have anything in common with me either. Maybe we weren't so different, after all.

We finally reached the narrow hallway of doors after walking up the endless staircase, and I saw that each door had names painted on it. I was surprised when I saw one with my name labeled on the white door in purple and blue.

She opened the door and let me walk in first. The room was beautiful; there were purple curtains with a purple bed. The bed had a white canopy on top and there was a large bookshelf. On top was my favorite book. I walked over and picked it up as she grinned widely. "Jared told me you loved that book. I really love it. I read it on Wednesday before you came. You'll find out that books make the time go easier."

Not once did she look at my forehead. I really liked her. I smiled to myself as I turned around and placed the book on the shelf. I couldn't believe Jared remembered, and why would he? Maybe he wasn't so bad or he just wanted me to feel comfortable while staying there. Beside the bookshelf, there was a large television set and a large movie selection. On the side, there was an iPod that was dark blue and headphones beside it. Beside the bed on the wall was an empty frame. It looked out of place, but I didn't mind. It was a part of the room.

"I feel like I'm at home," I told her and was stricken by how far away from my town I was. I missed my hometown but why? I was alone, and what good was that? I didn't go anywhere and until two days ago. I was without anyone at all. That was why it felt right. People make you feel comfortable just as my dad and mother made my home, home.

Holland watched with desolate eyes so I changed the subject. "How do you have so many books and movies? I'm so amazed," I expressed.

"Well, Gabe has a way of making things come and appear. He isn't magic, but he is a genius." Everyone seemed to associate the word genius with Gabe, but my thought was, arrogant asshole. She walked toward the panel that looked like an empty picture frame. "All right, what is something you want right now in your room?"

"Uh, I like candles," I said curiously.

She smiled. "I love the caramel kind." She looked distracted for a second before continuing. "All right, all you do is hold this button." She pointed to a red button on the side of the panel. "And say exactly what you want. From where and what it is. Watch. Caramel latte candle from Bath and Body Works."

As she said it, a huge candle appeared. She handed it to me.

"A lighter as well." She held down the panel and a lighter appeared.

"I know this seems like stealing, but Gabe pays for the things at the end of the month. He wants to get this into homes whenever this is all over. You won't even have to leave the house with this technology. He gets a bill from the stores we get things from. Gabe, Jared and I split our money to pay for everything, and I'm still in shock that we can afford everything. What is great is that they only can bill him from his computer so our location is still untraceable, because Gabe makes sure the computer is untraceable as well. So we are completely safe. It is amazing. He is amazing." She beamed to herself. I felt as if I was disturbing a thought and looked quickly away. She obviously had feelings for Gabe. And I didn't know how, but to each their own. "He invented this and Jared installed them. Jared wanted to be an engineer when he was in high school, just like I wanted to be a nurse. I had been in nursing school for like a month when Jared asked me to come here. I figured why not. Besides, what would be left of the world in a few years, anyway?"

She looked gloomy because of what she said or because it was the truth; I didn't know. I wanted to believe that the world would be just fine, but maybe that was wishful thinking. "I think you can save people," she said quietly, and I was startled. I felt pressure on me, and I felt as if I would collapse. "I'm sorry. I know that was too much. I know you don't even know anything, but I want to help you. Can you believe me when I say that?" I nodded, and she sighed with relief. "Good. I like you," she said as she nudged me.

"You're great, Holland. I love my room. Thank you so much," I said in a bashful tone.

"I really love designing, and I decorated every room and every hall. I love the kitchen and living room the best. Gabe wanted to see a little bit of black so I put black down this hall. He's so dark." She laughed to herself and then took a serious tone. "Hey, I know you're afraid about what you're doing here. But I want you to know that I won't let anything bad happen to you. I will make sure to keep Gabe in line. He likes to go overboard with things to find answers. Plus, we're girls. We've got to stick together."

She grabbed my hand and pulled me into a hug. I felt so at home and comfortable. I trusted Holland, but I was struck by something my father had just told me, *Don't trust everyone you met.* And I felt as if I found just the one not to trust.

Part Two: Jared

Chapter Twelve: What the hell, Gabe?

GABE FACED AWAY from me; he must have known I was pissed. He completely made Lena feel uncomfortable and didn't even try to make it right. He did this all the time. He made everyone belittled, because he was ultimately an asshole. I didn't think he would ever change, but still he was my best friend.

"Gabe?" He didn't respond, which pissed me off more. I picked up something off the table and chucked it at his head. He ducked and turned to me.

"You've gotten my attention." He took his glasses off to wipe sweat from his forehead. "You seem tense," he said accusingly. "You should probably calm down." He smirked, and I felt my hands shaking as my temper increased.

He knew exactly how to make me angry and I felt the rage burn inside me. I was ready to punch him in the face, but I knew he could do worse. Not because he was stronger, but because he was vindictive and cruel in other ways.

"Gabe, why did you do that to Lena?" I asked as calmly as possible.

"Do what?" He looked innocently at me.

"Look, you need to be nice to her and treat her better than that. Do you not remember who she is? She is kind of important to this whole thing. If you've forgotten, she could save the world. Holland was civil. What's your problem?" I stated.

"Let me just say I don't care if you're avoiding the truth. But I won't get close to her when she is like that." He rotated away from me again, and I clenched my fists so hard my nails dug into my hands, drawing blood.

"Gabe. What the hell are you talking about?" I asked with resentment.

"She's dead, man. She might as well be a walking corpse. Holland knows it, too. You're the only one who seems to be fooled by it. She is dying so fast she'll smell soon. She's not worth my time. No offense bro." His smile held no feeling, and he continued to work on his suit machine.

I tightened my hand into a fist and pushed all my weight into the center of his nose. His glasses knocked to the ground, but Gabe didn't seem to be affected whatsoever. He stood still and didn't budge from the force I put into the punch. My hand felt as if it went through glass, but it wasn't bleeding. I had punched many people, and I didn't hear the delicate crunch either like I normally did. I looked at him in suspicion. What happened to his face? It felt like stone now.

I didn't know why I was getting so defensive, but I couldn't help myself. I didn't understand why she affected me this way. Maybe she affected me because she was the one who could save us all.

He started to laugh as he yanked his glasses from the ground. After examining them carefully, he put them back on his face while continuing to cackle on, and I had no idea why. I just stared at him in disbelief. "What is so funny? What happened to you?" I asked in disgust and walked toward the steps.

"Look, I'm going to forget you just hit me, but she is dying. Also, it is funny because you're letting a girl take over your emotions. Do you really think she is worth this?" he asked in all seriousness.

"Yes. She is important to the entire human race." How could he not know how important she was to the entire world, or was he too egoistic to notice? "She is a huge part of this entire situation. Gabe, what is wrong with you?"

"Ha. Imagine living with Holland for a year and then talk to me about being different and whatever. My skin is hard now." He smiled as if he had heard some sick joke. His skin was thick, abnormally thick, and I didn't know why he didn't get hurt from my punch. Punches from me always led to a broken nose at the very least. What was wrong with him? I looked at him, and he dodged my glance quickly. "Honestly, we don't need her. We can figure this out without her," he told me confidently.

"Gabe, what has happened to you?" I asked.

"Nothing." He held my stare finally and I couldn't place what just happened. I shook my head and continued.

"I know the orders, and I know exactly what has to be done. She cannot die. She is the key to finding the solution. She has all the answers. I'm guessing they are locked away or maybe the answers are in her dad's laboratory. The night I got her, the lab was locked down. I don't understand why, but my guess was that the workroom is under her command. I couldn't find anything."

"You're going to have to find more answers. Does she know anything?"

"Not a thing." Gabe let out a frustrated sigh that irritated me, but I let it go. "Tell me about it," I said in agreement of his frustration.

"She has to. She's lying," he said quickly in a low voice.

"I thought so, too," I told him. "But, not a thing. We can try to see inside her mind with your mindreading stuff, but honestly, I don't think so."

"She seems useless. Let's get rid of her." I let that sink in, and I felt angry because what human should be thrown away like that, especially a life that was important to the entire human race. Even with the death toll rising, he wanted to kill someone else to add to it. Though no one would know, she was an asset to the cure of Dermadecatis.

"No," I shouted.

"Why?" He slinked toward me as a predator walking toward his prey.

"I think," I felt emotions bubbling in me and I tried to push them to the side, "she can give us information soon. She might have value to us. If she was given the disease like this, they obviously want to control her." I didn't want to admit how important she would be whenever she figured out the truth.

"That is a good point. She must be of importance or she is just like the rest of the world. They just want to control everyone. It's a power thrill." He looked up to me with a peculiar look. "Do you, maybe, have feelings for this girl? Is that why you think she is of vital importance?" He sneered, and I suddenly felt nervous. My stomach clenched at the possibility that he might be right, but that would be impossible. I returned the

Antidote

smirk. "No. I know the mission, and I know feelings, as you say, would get in the way."

"She isn't ugly. If she were healthy, I would make her mine," he remarked wisely.

I felt jealously sweep over me, but I shoved it aside. "Well, I would like her healthy or not, but she's annoying. Have at it." I winced at my words. I didn't want Gabe to have her, and a sick feeling passed through me as he smiled. He would probably try, but Lena wouldn't fall for it. "Are you going to help or not?" I asked to distract him and myself. Gabe stared me down for a second before answering.

"Well, I don't know where to start honestly. Holland is up there with her. I'm sure she is trying to figure out the severity of it. She'll probably do some tests. If her brain is affected enough, she'll have mood swings and probably have problems with speech. I don't know how bad it is or how much she's fighting it."

"How did she get this, anyway? I have no answers. I was so sure that I knew where the disease came from and how it was contracted, and I avoided it. Then one day she's sick and has the disease. He really out did himself, don't you think? Lena's father and I had this all figured out, and now I don't know where to start to figuring this out."

"Sebastian did know what he was talking about." Gabe nodded in approval before he continued. "First off, you need to tell Lena the truth about everything."

"No, Gabe," I said fiercely. "I'm still working on her trusting me. Would it be wise to tell her something to completely lose her trust?"

"Fine, but you need to tell her what will happen to her if she doesn't get help soon." I didn't answer. I knew what the right thing was to do, but I didn't know what she would think of me after that. I didn't want her to find out the truth without me telling her myself.

"Ah. Jared." He hesitated. "It's a little worse than what we thought. Her dad might have suspected what was going to happen, but he didn't know what they were planning." He walked to the computer and started typing until the television turned on.

The scene was a burning gas station, the very one we were at. On the side of the video, the newsman was no longer in the picture. Gabe's voice interrupted my thoughts. "This was behind the scenes. Of course I found a way into the system." I could hear the smile in his voice. "The government cleaned this up fast, but I got there first. Undetected, I might add," he gloated.

"Of course you did." He laughed, but I did not because the picture before me was frightening. Four people, well, superhuman people, were in the back of the video. They rammed their bodies into the side of the gas station and were torn apart by a sort of magic force, but they didn't bleed. Their severed figures were lying uselessly on the ground while three more people flew through the air. One person ripped a car door off its hinges in the parking lot and tossing it through the gas station window. The frame halted as a person paused in place in the middle of the picture with a blue glow around them. The glowing man flew through the air, grazing the top of the gas station as it completely exploded. The screen went fuzzy, and Gabe took the picture away.

"What in the hell was that?" was all I could manage to say.

"Well, my friend. The camera was destroyed, and no one has seen this film but Holland, you, whoever deleted the footage and I. The worst part is that I have no clue what is going on. My guess is someone has found a way to get complete mind control over these people. Not with the disease, but with the cure. Whenever they do something wrong, such as not capture who should be captured, they are made to self-destruct because they proved themselves useless. There is one man I have seen a million times the past few days." A picture popped up on the screen of a boy with brown hair and black eyes. He had his normal hard expression. It was Joseph. I felt my teeth clench together as I let the memories of the past few days swirl through me.

"Let me get this straight, he has found complete mind control over them," I retorted unsurely.

"That is essentially the idea, and I don't know how to stop them. I can find a real cure for Lena and the others, but I don't know how to stop the mind control. Either I find a cure or Lena is going to die. Or she'll be controlled forever by them."

"I can't let that happen. I won't let that happen. She can't be made into a mindless girl who kills innocent people," I said mainly to myself.

The door suddenly burst open, and Holland walked swiftly down the steps.

"Where is Lena?" I asked in a hard tone.

"Oh, I gave her up for female sacrifice." She simpered, but I didn't return it so she continued. "No, she is cooking a cherry pineapple turnover cake. Thank god. I don't know desserts. Lighten up Jared." Holland winked at me. "Did you show him the tape?" She directed this question to Gabe.

"Yes. Just now," Gabe answered calmly. I didn't feel calm, I felt like the world was falling apart around me, and I couldn't help Lena.

"What do you think, Jar? It's pretty insane. I have a different theory than Gabe." She turned to Gabe. "Look, we need to crack this baby open. I felt her head like I told you I would, and I felt a bump. I think they have inserted the disease and they connected a chip ahead of time to make it easier."

"Easier for what?" I asked uneasily.

"When they turn them into robots," she said in a matter-of-fact way. "Especially Lena's case. They want to turn her into one quickly when they receive her so the chip is already located there."

Gabe slammed his hand down and looked at Holland with a look of intensity before speaking. "I swear to all that is holy, if you tell Lena about the chip, I will kill you. Don't you doubt it?"

"Oh, shut up. I'm not a dumbass like you." She wasn't afraid of Gabe, which I really admired. Gabe wasn't someone I wanted to mess with. She hopped back up onto the table. "Look, Jared, I know you don't want to hear it, but Gabe isn't always right. They are robots or they are given the qualities of robots because, what 'mind controlled' human is going to fly through shit and break things with their hands and glow? None." She emphasized the mind controlled to show that Gabe wasn't right. "They are using mind control by making them superhuman. AKA robots. I'm right, and you know it, Jared."

She was right. There was no other explanation that I could see. I knew one thing for sure, and that was I wasn't going to let Lena become a robot. Not when she was of vital importance and maybe a little for my own good. I hated to admit it, but she was already someone I cared for, but I couldn't tell either of them that.

"When do we start with Lena?" I asked with a frustrated groan.

"Excellent." Holland clapped her hands together.

"Holland, you need to shut it." Holland pouted as Gabe revolved back to stare at me. "Jared, we'll start whenever I figure out what I need to do," Gabe told me.

Holland scowled at him and twisted to me. "He thinks he is too good for this, but I will do it myself if he doesn't want to help. I have a few ideas of my own. First, I think we need to look in there."

"Look in where?" I asked in ambiguity.

"Well, her arm or her brain. I think the most beneficial place would be the brain, but Lena has to agree," Holland told me in confidence.

"No. I won't let you," I told her angrily.

She shrugged softly, and said, "Then she is as good as dead." She looked past me and then to the floor.

Gabe stepped forward to cover Holland from my view, and I was thankful because I probably would have said something terrible. "Would you feel better if I performed the procedure? Holland can cut her where she felt the lump and that'll be it."

Holland looked at Gabe with an, *Are you serious?* look that I could see as I peeked past his shoulder. I talked directly to her. "I don't care who does it, but maybe Holland wouldn't try to kill her if she's useless." Gabe winced, but I knew he didn't mind hearing the truth. "Gabe, you can do it, but promise me you won't kill her under any circumstances, no matter how you feel."

Gabe nodded his agreement. Holland chattered on, breaking the hostile silence. "I wasn't going to do it, but if he refused, I would have, but probably sloppy." She smiled. "Let's go eat. I made chicken pie for dinner, and Lena's making our dessert. Come on."

I followed her. Gabe actually followed us, which was amazing, because he probably never left the lab. He shut the lights off, and I walked in front of him. Just before he shut the door, I watched him whisper a command to the door to lock it.

Chapter Thirteen: The Bad Guys Are Always the Good Guys First

I FOLLOWED THE smell into the kitchen. I walked in and saw Lena smiling widely. "I love cooking. I'm so glad I can be useful right now," she said softly.

"It smells wonderful," Holland told Lena as she put her arm around Lena's arm. Lena's eyes widened and a smile danced on her lips. Her gaze grazed over mine and I felt as if she purposely avoided eye contact, which bothered me. I didn't know why.

Lena was different than any girl I had ever met. She yelled back, and she didn't take things off anyone. She had darkness all through her face, but when her eyes shined through, she was stunning. I didn't see this before she was sick and that bothered me. I had gotten to know Lena in the past few days, and it was weird to see how much she meant to me already.

Holland started laughing and talking with Lena. I sat in the chair by the table and stared between them. Gabe sat beside me with his iPad propped up. Holland was great at making people feel welcome. She was like the sister that I needed and was always there for me. I remembered when I introduced Gabe to Holland. Holland hated Gabe. He told her that he liked her hair, and she felt offended because everything he said sounded sarcastic. That was just how he was. Everything came off as rude whenever Gabe said it. Eventually you get used to Gabe and his ways. Even I hated Gabe when I first met him.

"So. Tell me about yourselves," Lena said, breaking the silence to Gabe.

He peered up through his glasses and pushed them on his nose. Just like the dork he was.

"You first," she said, pointing to him. Holland clasped her hands together at full attention. I bit down a laugh and smiled at him. I batted my eyes to show I was listening. He frowned.

"There isn't much to know about me," he said and looked back down to his iPad.

"Tell me anyway," Lena said with a smile.

Gabe looked up once more and sighed. He closed the iPad. "Fine. I was born and raised in a small town in California by my mother. My dad quit my mom and me when I was not even two months old. I was an only child, like yourself." Lena smiled and nodded for him to go on. "I met Jared at the age of five. We were really best buds. We managed to get to fourth grade together when they decided my brain was too advanced for the fourth grade. I was thrown into eleventh grade at age eleven. Imagine my surprise when I saw girls didn't look like the other fourth graders anymore." He rolled his eyes, and Lena let out a giggle. He was really getting into this.

"I graduated high school when I was twelve. I wasn't really someone who fit in, which sucked. I kind of felt like my childhood was taken from me. But lucky me, I had Jared." He paused and looked to Holland who was beaming at him. I felt as if I was disturbing something personal. Something I didn't miss seeing. "And I had Holland." He said her name as if he were reading a scripture. He quickly continued. "Went to college until I was seventeen. I was going to get a PhD, but look where we are now." He sighed.

"I was outside one afternoon. I was tending to the vegetable garden I had outside my house. It was summertime. My mother had the screen door open. She was telling me how proud she was of me for almost being a doctorate. I was proud, too. I wanted it more than I wanted anything else. I still want those things." He looked dazed for a second, then continued. "The TV came on. You know how that goes. When there is a bad alert, every TV in the world turns on. Every single one, and you better be glad you're listening. Isaac." He said it and I felt sadness. His eyes closed momentarily. Lena missed it, though, because she was looking down. She was probably remembering her own memories. "Isaac was dying. I like to call it the first case ever of this disgusting, bullshit disease and the one that stopped me from being a doctor. The one that stopped me from everything, but that doesn't matter. I wouldn't be here with you all."

He stopped and took a deep breath. "I rushed inside to my mom. I told her we had to get out of there. We had to find some place safe. It was too late for her. Lena," he said softly, and I knew he knew she understood loss like this. "My mother was dying already. Surprisingly not from the disease, like you probably assumed. She was a slow woman. She had multiple disorders. She told me that she would slow us down. She wasn't worth the time or space. She told me to find safety without her. She told me to leave her. And I did." He shook his head.

"I will never know if she could have survived if I wouldn't have left that day to find Jared. Jared told me he always had a safe house waiting for loved ones." He looked down at the table. "I still don't know what became of her. I still don't know if she died from the disease or from her disorders. I don't know anything about her now." He hung his head low. "This is why I didn't really want to talk." Lena reached a hand across the table to touch his. It wasn't a romantic gesture. It was more like to say, *"I am here for you. I understand you."* He peered up and gave a sad smile.

"Holland's turn," he said with a sniffle. Lena smiled and gently patted his hand before pulling away. She turned to Holland and nudged her with her arm.

"Okay. Where to start." She paused and made a face as if she remembered something sour. "I guess I can start by saying I have no idea who my parents were. I had fifty brothers and sisters and I loved them deeply." Lena looked at her with a confused look. She laughed. "My foster mom was named Mrs. Juliet."

Lena nodded, and said, "Ohhh."

"I was left on the doorstep when I was a day old. Or so Mrs. Juliet told me. Skip forward, I was never adopted. I always dreamed of going to school, so Mrs. Juliet decided to take me and a few other kids to school. Guess where I ended up." She laughed and looked between the two boys.

"I entered the kindergarten class and there comes Jared. His hair was a mess. I honestly think the first word I said was, 'Your hair looks like crap.'" She laughed hard, and Lena began to laugh with her.

"Honestly, I am sure that is what happened," I said with a chuckle.

She smiled before turning back to Lena. "Jared and I were instant friends. Gabe was out sick that day, and oh boy, the next day, he was so angry with Jared. He said, 'What is wrong with you? You picked a girlfriend?'" she said as she impersonated Gabe. Gabe rolled his eyes and stuck his tongue out at her as if he were a child.

"They bickered like two girls. I hated Gabe for a long time. He told me he hated my hair, and I told him I hated his sarcastic attitude. Still true story." She smiled at him longingly. "My story about the day of Isaac is a little different. I was with Jared."

I felt a tinge of fear. I knew the story well. I hoped they wouldn't tell Lena more than she needed to know. "Jared and I were studying at the local library. We were seventeen, but unlike Gabe we still were in high school." She sighed. "I wanted to be a nurse like I told you before. I was going to go all the way, here actually, in North Carolina, to a nursing school. Jared and I were whispering, and the librarian was telling us to hush. That's when the only TV in the place started blaring. The sound was awful." It was like she was being transported in time. "I saw his face on the screen, so Jared and I rushed over. We both," she stopped herself, "knew Isaac. He was from our classes." She stopped talking, but Lena still looked to her oblivious. "Anyway, the disease was born the moment Isaac died. Jared and I stood frozen in the library while chaos erupted. Next thing I knew, we were bolting from town. We came to see Gabe and we got him to come with us. He told us he was leaving to find us, too. We were gone."

"I know it sounds silly that everyone freaked out. The thing is, it started in our town. It was our outbreak. You were in town. What did you go through?" Holland asked softly.

Lena leaned forward to begin talking, but instead clutched her stomach as her other hand grabbed a hold of the side of the counter. She ran toward the hallway, and I ran after her before I could stop myself. Holland tagged behind Lena, following as close as she could to her. Holland and I both stopped at the door as we heard Lena gag and vomit. I walked in, and she put a hand up. In between her heaves, she got out the word "Holland." I felt a knot in my stomach, but I knew I didn't have a right to comfort her. I wished I didn't want to comfort her.

Holland walked in behind me and had an unopened toothbrush. She smiled to me gloomily as she closed the door. I stood there, trying to listen to their conversation, but then I remembered the rooms were soundproof.

I walked back to Gabe and put my hands on the counter sides. He didn't meet my eyes, and I knew why. He took his glasses off and wiped his forehead.

"Jared," he said just audible for me to hear.

"I know, I know. What can we do?"

"We need to start now. She's very sick. She's going to die if we don't do something now. This is serious." His eyes were full of contempt.

I didn't say anything. I had come to like her over the past few days. I didn't want to lose her.

"Jared, she is not strong enough to withstand the disease. They must have given her an extra dose or they really did put a chip in to enhance it like Holland suggested, because this is the sign of the people that are about to die. She is very sick. If it's bad enough, there will be blood in that. Holland will know what to look for. It's better that Holland went in there because she knows exactly what to look for. I mean we've been locked up in here for so long, all we do is look for what causes the disease and what it is."

I didn't meet his eyes and said all I could manage. "Yeah."

"Look, Holland and I have been trying to figure out how they get the disease in them. We thought it was in the food. Then we thought maybe it was airborne or in the water, but I know it isn't because only a few people have gotten it in a population. So I want you to tell me everything you did before she got sick. There has to be answers in what you did."

"Well, before she got sick, we were chased by Joseph and his clan."

"Ah, Joseph, the first cure right?" He laughed, and I felt myself getting flustered.

"Why are you laughing?" I asked, bewildered.

"Well, the cure is turning them into mindless freaks, so I don't think it was Joseph chasing you, but the 'other kind.'" He added his signature air quotes, and I smiled. It was good to see some things never changed.

"All right, the 'other kind,'" I mocked Gabe, "chased us down the highway and into the gas station. They chased us out of her house. We slept in her dad's lab, but I don't think there was anything harmful there because he wouldn't have left harmful things there with Lena. I told you I looked for things there, but I came up short. But anyway, we got in a wreck, and she had to get stitches. We escaped the hospital because they found her there, too. Then we stayed in a hotel, and she was sick after she ate pancakes. She showed me her arm that day. Her forehead started to rot after that. It might have been sooner, because she had a bandage over it. I have no idea what happened for her to get this."

Gabe stood to his feet slowly and began pacing; this was something he did when he was on to something. "When did they start chasing and finding you?"

I told him that they always knew where we were. I even told him about the dead hotel managers, and I told him how Lena was fine until the girl from the gas station pointed it out.

"Where did Lena get stitches?" He leaned down to the table and stared at me with piercing eyes.

"Her forehead." I stopped in place and got up slowly. I covered my mouth and almost howled. My vision blurred as the realization washed over me.

Gabe just stood shaking his head. "Yes, they led her right in. They hurt her and then they put the disease in her." He wobbled his head fiercely for a long time. "On the bright side, we know how they contract the disease now. I wonder if we can stop them. I could send out a warning to the world to not trust doctors. Who would believe us, though?" He ranted on, but I was unfocused. I couldn't believe it. I put my head in my hands. The hospital, the doctors were killing innocent people.

Gabe spoke softly. "What should we do? If the good guys of the world are the bad guys, we'll have no one to help us find the real cure." He watched me. "I'll have to find the cure alone. They are injecting them with the disease; maybe I can take it out or something. I just don't know how to do that, Jared." He seemed lost, but I knew he could figure this out. If anyone could, it would be Gabe.

"Do whatever you can. I want her to live. I don't want her to get controlled." He turned to me with suspicious eyes, and I knew what he was really thinking and it was "why should you care?"

The bathroom opened, and Holland stepped out with Lena leaning against her. "Lena said to take out the dessert. It's done. She is both silly and considerate. We're going to change her clothes. She said she feels better, and she's hungry." She smiled to us, but the smile froze on her lips and went no farther on her face. She appeared frightened, which made me worry.

I heard the door to Lena's room close and Holland's high heels hitting the floor as she rushed to us. "Gabe, I couldn't see anything, but I know this. The blood is black. There was black all over her lips." She cringed. "She is rotting big time and fast," she frantically whispered. "What are we going to do? This is worse than I thought. I know she's dying very fast. She's not holding food and you can see her ribs. It's really scary, and the smell." She wrinkled her nose. "I sprayed in there, don't worry," she said before Gabe could protest. "She is really trying to make Jared not see how bad it is. That's why she asked me in. She told me why she didn't want you in there. If you were wondering." She held her arms out. I hugged her, and she whispered into my ear. "I know you must really care for her. Maybe she doesn't know, but I do." I pulled away and looked at her in shock. She just nodded in encouragement. I didn't care for her like that. Or did I? I wished I could make sense of this.

"We need to start tonight." Gabe spoke up, and I death glared him.

"Ask her. Don't decide for her. Her fate is decided already so let her decide one thing," I told him heatedly.

The door creaked open, and I heard her feet softly hit the floor. We all tried to act normal. Holland even flattened her hair down.

"I'm sorry everyone. Holland, do you want to wait and eat later? I'm so sorry. Thank you for being in there with me." She started blushing, and it was a nice change to not see her frustrated. The color on her cheeks seemed to awaken her soul, and she looked more beautiful in that moment.

Holland walked to her and pulled Lena into a long embrace. "I'll be here for you. Now that I have seen that, I can take anything."

She beamed to Holland. Lena needed someone accepting. I wasn't the one Lena wanted to be accepting of her.

"Is anyone hungry?" Lena called from behind Holland. Holland shook her head fast, and Lena snickered.

Gabe spoke up. "Lena, how about we all sit and talk a little, and if we get hungry, we can eat. It smells wonderful." He searched our faces and turned to walk toward the kitchen. We all followed. I spoke up.

"Eat man, I don't want to, but you can. It might make me hungry," I told him, and Gabe eagerly grabbed a bowl and dug into the chicken pie, obviously unaffected by the turn of events. He sat and let out a sigh when he tried it.

"Okay let's talk," Holland said in a tired way to Gabe.

"Well," Gabe began as he took another bite. "It's going to be hard to fix you. The hospital inserted the disease inside you. That's how you contracted it to begin with."

"The hospital?" Lena asked silently. "That can't be."

Gabe threw up a hand to silence her. "Holland, Jared and I are going to do everything we can to get the disease out of you before we have to do something drastic or before this gets any worse," he said indifferently.

Lena gave all her attention, but her eyes widened in fear. "Am I going to die?"

We all stopped in place, and Gabe slowly put down his food. He got up and kneeled to Lena. He took her hands. Obviously taking up on his proposition to win her over. "I will do everything I can to make you better. We all will. You are apart of our little family now. You will have to bear with me and let me try all these things. I will not let them take you away." I was in shock. I felt frustration build up inside me. He heard how Holland said I cared for her. I knew he had even if she talked quietly.

She smiled, and I saw her eyes were beginning to look glassy. "Who would take me away?" she asked reluctantly.

Gabe looked slowly to me, and I nodded. Lena searched my face before she turned back to Gabe. "Lena, they will take you and take full control of your mind." She looked shocked, but her face fell.

"How would they do that, Gabe?"

Holland spoke up this time. "We aren't sure yet, but we have theories about this cure that they're giving out. I think, no, *we* think, they will insert a robotic arm into you that soon spreads to your brain and takes over your mind. I believe that—" Gabe cut her off quickly with a look, and she stopped speaking abruptly.

Lena burst into tears, and Holland sauntered to her. I stayed seated because I was afraid as well. I couldn't let her see me upset. She might see that I had feelings for her, and what good would that be for either of us? "We won't let it get there," Holland reassured Lena.

"How do you know?" Lena asked through her tears.

"We don't know that, but we won't do it unless it's your last breath," Holland told her.

"What if I would rather die?" she asked calmly.

"Gabe believes there is a way to bring them back. Bring the robo—" She stopped again when she looked at Gabe. "Bring the people back to their human ways. So if it came down to it, we would try to find a way to bring you back," Holland explained to Lena.

"But what if you can't bring me back?" she enquired delicately, and I got up this time.

"Lena, we are going to do absolutely everything we can. We can make this better if you let us do whatever it takes." Lena looked to me, but her eyes were searching and distant. Maybe I insulted her one too many times. I felt angry with myself for taking all my anger out on her.

She didn't respond, but looked to Gabe. "When do we start?"

Gabe smiled to Holland and I. I just nodded curtly. Holland quickly met my gaze, and I could see myself in her face. Fear.

Chapter Fourteen: When is Enough, Enough for you?

LENA AND HOLLAND cleaned the kitchen, and I sat across from Gabe. He continued to stare me down as I chewed slowly on the cake Lena made for us. His gaze hadn't left my face yet, so I felt a little aggravated.

"Something to say, Gabe?" I asked irritably. Holland glanced back, and she had the same intrigued look on her face that Gabe had. What was up? Lena was busy cleaning and didn't seem to notice the tension.

"You knew what was going to happen, didn't you?" Gabe asked accusingly. "You knew what was going to happen to the world and you didn't do a damn thing." Gabe was shaking with anger, and I felt myself getting pissed. Lena was in the room with us. She could hear him.

"We can take this out to another room. I'm not discussing this here." My gaze swept over to Lena, and his followed mine. Why did he want to talk about this all of a sudden?

"How'd you know? Was it her dad or someone else who told you?" He was very careful not to mention who I didn't want him to, but he was still provoking me. He wanted to make me look like the bad guy in front of Lena. "Jared, be honest with us. We've been investing a lot of time, trying to figure this out and you knew the answers all along. That is such bullshit. How can we trust you when you do this?"

That was it. I slammed my fist hard onto the table, and that was when Lena turned to watch. "Shut the hell up. You don't know what you're talking about." I got up and slammed the seat into the table. I walked out of the room, and I felt three pairs of eyes on me.

I was getting so livid with Gabe lately. He just knew how to make me furious, and made me feel helpless whenever he accused me of things. I couldn't help what I knew, and I certainly couldn't help that I had feelings for the girl with all the answers.

I heard hushed whispers, but I went to my room and slammed the door, locking it behind me. There was a brisk knock. I didn't open it. The door opened anyway and Holland walked in freely.

"Jared, we need to talk," Holland said quietly.

"How did you get in?" I asked irritated.

"I designed the doors, remember?" Holland retorted quickly.

"What are we talking about that is so important that you have to barge in?" Holland's eyes blazed, and her face turned a dark pink in frustration. I gave her my full attention. "Okay. What?"

"You need to tell her, no, you must tell her. How can she trust you when you have a lie hanging over your head?"

"Holland, I can't. I already told Gabe. She won't trust me. Don't you and Gabe share a brain? You should've known that already." Her face fell, but quickly recovered.

"Yes, she'll trust you even less if you don't tell her now. If she finds out in a different way other than you, that will just make things worse. Gabe might be telling her as we speak. I wouldn't put it past him, Jared. And you don't need to take your anger out on me. I didn't do anything."

"Holland, I understand the severity of the situation, but I don't want to lose the little trust we have so far.

And if Gabe tells her, then I will kick him out. This is my house, remember? I built this with my mother before you two came along." Holland just stood in place as her eyes looked blank and unchanging, not pitying me and not wanting to pity me.

"Kick me out too then. He goes, I go." I looked on in disbelief. I didn't want to lose both my friends.

"Holland, never mind. I just hope he isn't telling her." I shook my head. Holland put too much trust in Gabe.

She didn't seem fazed by what I said so she continued. "Jar. If she is someone you care about, and I sense that you do care for her, then you need to start off with honesty. With honest intentions." She walked slowly over. "You will lose her. She is dying, and she is dying fast. She'll have to be sent to them if we don't get this together now. If we don't join forces, she is going to die. You'll lose her that way. Wouldn't you rather save her and have her hate you than lose her for good?"

"You're right." I paused and stared around the room. It was really beautiful how Holland fixed it. My mother began designing the house, but died before she could fix up one room. Holland fixed all of the rooms with my mother's drawn-up plans and added her own flare to it. I never told Lena about my family, and she never asked. Maybe if she hadn't gotten sick at the dinner table, she would have asked me. The room was lightly dimmed because the working lamp was burning out that sat in the corner. I didn't like that there weren't any windows, but we were underground so it couldn't be helped. The blank picture frame that every room held was like a window for me. Holland was a smart girl when it came to all of this. "I will have to tell her. But I will tell her at the right time."

"Why not now?" she asked suspiciously. Her eyes squinted as if she were thinking hard.

"I don't want her to stop looking at me the same way. Even when she doesn't like me, she has a glow when she looks at me. Can't you understand that? I want to fix her. In every way." I surprised myself with my honesty. Holland just stood there, shaking her head.

"It is up to you, but if I were her, I would want to know. It would be easier to forgive you. Just think about it. Come out when you're ready." She turned to leave and locked the door as she entered the hallway.

I watched the door to make sure no one else wanted to come in and slowly opened the picture frame. I was sure they didn't forget that I made this house, too. I opened the safe hidden behind the empty frame and inside sat the picture of my seven-year-old self with my father. God knew I missed him. I wished he was the same man, but he wasn't. I could fake it and be his friend so I could save Lena. But I didn't think I could stomach it. He was a liar and a murderer. It could never be the same with him, and he knew it. I had to find a way to make him not take Lena, though.

I couldn't tell her, but I guess she had a right to know. She had a right to know that she could be murdered at any moment or taken over.

There was a soft rasp. I shut the frame and opened the door. Lena stood with a smug look on her face. "Come in," I told her. Her hands were placed behind her back as she stood on her heels.

"Holland told me to come talk to you. What's going on?" I guess Holland decided to take matters in her own hands. I moved out of the way to let her inside. "It's a long story, so I would sit down. Before I tell you, I want you to know that I wanted to tell you about it, but I didn't trust you yet. Not like I do now. I know you don't trust me, and I understand that. I haven't been the nicest person."

She looked afraid, but nodded in agreement. She was forgiving and understanding even if it meant something bad for her. I continued, "Well, I know exactly what is going on with these people. I've known all along." She looked hurt. I told her the one piece of information that I kept locked inside me. "I know this because my father is the man in charge."

Chapter Fifteen: I Wonder If She'll Ever Look At Me The Same

SHE DIDN'T LOOK at me for about ten minutes. I sat in silence. I could tell she felt betrayed because her eyes watered up as if she would cry. She always made a strange sound to calm herself. She repeatedly grabbed the necklace around her neck. It was something she often did, and I wondered of its significance to her. "Please go on," she told me finally.

"I'm not with my dad. I do not work for him or with him. I know I should have told you sooner. I really don't know why I tried to keep it from you. I thought it was the only way to keep you safe." I hesitated and tried my best to not look at the bandage over her head. She seemed to notice because she reached up slowly and shaded her forehead.

I wanted to tell her not to cry, but she did. She pulled slowly so the bandage was off. There was no way to explain it other than being devastating. Even when she was like this, her eyes still shined hazel under the black mass on her forehead. The right eye, where the cut was rotting the most, was turning a gray color. The thing was, you could see inside her head now. It was black and there was dried up blood on the outside of the hole. She was literally rotting from the inside out. Her arm was doing the same thing, but instead of a hole, there was just black growing along her skin all the way to her shoulder. I was afraid if I touched her that her forearm would just fall off. It was as if her body was decaying after death.

They were destroying bodies until they had nothing else to do but go back to the hospital. Even if you knew where the disease came from like Lena knew now. The difference between the others and us was that we were going to fight. We were going to make sure that she had her body and full control of her mind. I wasn't going to give her up without a fight.

"Lena, do you feel terrible or do you just not feel this?"

"It feels like someone is inside me, slowly destroying me. It's most painful at night. I have dreams about weird things. I throw up blood so much, and sometimes it comes out black, which is nasty. I'm sorry if I gross you out. This is the most pain I've been in, in my entire life. Sometimes the air feels toxic to me, and I want to stop breathing. It hurts my lungs, and I can just feel myself dying. My heart stops beating sometimes, but I don't die. And it hurts to shower. Each time I do, the hole in my head gets blacker. It is so disgusting. Why did my mom and dad die? My dad died to protect me from the disease. Look where I am now. I feel helpless and useless. I want to protect you, Gabe and Holland from this. I think if I died then it would be okay. You guys could stay here and be safe." She looked away from me, tears trickling down from her eyes.

"Lena, I want to tell you something, and I don't want you to let it make you feel differently about the situation," I said sincerely. My heart was beating in my chest. My ears began to buzz.

"Okay," she said as tears fell lightly.

I grabbed her face and turned it to mine. We were so close to each other, I could feel each breath she took. "You make me forget my troubles. You make me feel alive. I have come to really care for you." I hesitated, searching her face for any fear. She smiled encouragingly, and I continued, "That's why I don't want anything to happen to you. That's why I have been so crazy to get you help from Gabe. I didn't even realize it before until I saw you were sick. Then again, I think I knew, before I knew you were sick, that I cared about you."

She stopped crying and gripped my hand and beamed. She put her lips to my hand and laughed.

"What is so funny?" I asked defensively.

"I'm just happy. I've been trying to figure you out. You seem so unattainable, and here you are. Here you are, and you like me. I'm dying, and this is so selfish of you. Selfish of you because I don't have time and you want that time. No one has ever found me appealing, and if they have, I haven't returned it. I have known it for a while that I care for you, too, but I didn't want to face it. I don't want to be angry that my time with you is cut short. That isn't fair." She seemed angry so I grabbed her chin and pushed it up.

"We'll make the most of our time if you don't make it." Her eyes watered. "But that's the thing. You will make it. I believe in you. I know we haven't known each other long, and I was an ass, but you've made me feel so happy."

She never dropped her gaze and calmly spoke. "It sucks that it's under these circumstances, but I'm glad I'm here with you. Finally."

We held each other's gaze. I lifted my lips to hers and melted into the shape of her mouth. I felt myself escaping the world. We held each other in this embrace for a while and then I left her lips. I held her in my arms, and we stared up at the ceiling in complete bliss. We fell asleep holding each other.

I was awoken by a curling scream. I began to panic and saw that Lena was frantically walking around the room while holding her hands to her eyes.

"What is it? What's wrong?" I screamed. Her eyes began to roll to the back of her head, and I took off running for the door.

I opened it, and the sound of Lena screaming exploded into the hallway.

"Holland! Gabe!" I shouted. In a blink of an eye, Holland stood before me, pushing her way past me.

"What happened? Did you do something?" Gabe asked to me accusingly as he approached the room.

"Look at her eyes," I told him quietly.

He walked in, and Holland had dropped to her knees beside Lena, talking calmly. "Sweetie, show me what's wrong. What is wrong?" She rubbed her hair, and instantly Lena got quiet. Holland began saying soothing words to Lena until Lena closed her eyes and took a huge breath.

"Now, tell me what's wrong." She tried again.

"My eyes were burning. I was crying and then I don't know what happened. I felt like my eyes were going out of my head." I wondered why she had been crying, then I remembered when she said her dreams scared her sometimes.

The pain she was in and the strength she had was what made me feel so powerful. I would help Lena. We would all three make Lena better. We had to. She deserved the best treatment and medicine.

It was as if Holland heard me in her mind. "We are going to fight for you if you fight for you. We can do everything we can to fix you, sweetie. Let us try."

There was silence for a long time, and Gabe paced back and forth. I knew he was nervous about watching someone die. It probably reminded him of his mother dying of a disease and he wasn't there to help her get better.

"Okay, I will fight if you all promise to fight, too."

We all nodded, and I heard Gabe say, "I promise."

I stared at him in amazement. He must have been under the spell that was Lena Alona. She was loveable, and sometimes I found myself forgetting that Gabe was a human himself and could feel emotions. He had grown to like Lena in just a few hours.

"When do we start?" Lena repeated the words from Gabe earlier. She rubbed her eyes, but Holland held her hands in her own.

"Now," Gabe told her with confidence.

Chapter Sixteen: Just Kill Me Now

LENA WAS LYING across the table in the lab. She looked frightened. Her gaze flickered to mine, and she gave an encouraging smile each time mine met hers. It was hard to rely on Gabe, but it wasn't hard to believe in Holland, and I knew Lena trusted her. I could understand why it was hard to trust someone who was hot one minute and cold the next. It baffled Lena. He was still that way with Holland and me, but we had grown used to it.

Lena continuously shook on the table from her nerves.

"Are you doing okay?" I asked. She had to be nervous. I didn't want her to be scared.

"Don't worry about me." She gave her fakest smile. "The table is just a little cold." Holland didn't meet her gaze, and after a few moments, Lena closed her eyes.

She slowly moved up as the tabletop transformed into a seat for her from the button Holland pushed. Holland approached Lena while holding a tube, and I stiffened.

"Okay. This will numb the pain for the most part." Holland bit down on her lip as she said this. "It's going to hurt." Lena opened her eyes to Holland. Holland nodded to her in reassurance. Lena laid her head back down and tensed up. Holland rubbed a white, goopy ointment onto her forehead. She closed her eyes as she got to the hole in Lena's head. I didn't think it was because she was repulsed, but instead she might have been scared to let Lena see how badly it hurt her to see her hurt. Holland was like that. She didn't want to see anyone hurt on her accord.

I was lucky to have spent as much time as I had with Lena, which still wasn't enough for me. I wished I'd had more time with her. She made my soul wake up when she walked into the room and even when she was sick, or close to dying, she woke my heart up when she spoke. I didn't know my feelings were this strong, but once I finally admitted them to myself, the emotions flooded through me.

Lena left her eyes closed as Holland lathered her forehead with the ointment. Gabe paced back and forth like he always did. He didn't seem as confident as normal, which worried me.

Holland warned her that the needle was long and would sting a lot. Lena didn't as much as jump when Holland stuck the needle in to numb her even more. Holland held her hand, but Lena seemed to feel nothing in her body anymore. Her hand went limp as it fell to her side and out of Holland's hand. I jumped up and ran to her. I placed mine over hers and asked if she was okay. Then I realized she wasn't breathing anymore. She wasn't moving at all.

"Is she okay?" I half shrieked.

Holland didn't seem to hear me. She turned around and spoke quietly. "She's been put to sleep, so she doesn't feel this." She turned to Gabe and nodded. He walked to the table and started typing feverously.

"Then why isn't she breathing?" I shouted over the typing.

"Listen again. Her heartbeat should be back now," Gabe called back carelessly. "Damn, I wish we had an EKG machine," he muttered to himself.

I moved my hand to her neck to feel her pulse. Nothing. I closed my eyes and prayed it came back. I jumped in place as I felt her heartbeat beneath my hands. She looked peaceful, and I was glad that she wouldn't experience any pain from this. I kissed her hand and I found Gabe still typing. "What are we doing?" I asked calmly. "How can I help?"

"We have to get this inside her head." He picked up a wire without looking up from his typing. "It has to go in until it touches where the hospital inserted the disease. It won't be easy at all." Gabe pointed to the end of the log wire where a tiny round shape was. "This here is a camera. On this big screen, we'll watch for the blackness. On the inside there should be a red dot where they inserted the disease. In the camera, I built a zapper, as I call it. I'm going to try to zap the target site, thus getting rid of the disease. Hopefully. Sounds simple, but it really isn't. We could destroy something in the frontal lobe. She could lose memories or her personality could change just like Phineas Gage. I think that's the point of putting the disease in her forehead because they want them to forget their memories and not have the same personality as before." He stopped talking as he typed something again. "Jared, I would just try to hold the wire up so it goes in at the right angle. Holland, you know what to do. Guide it in, and I will work on the zapping when the time comes. Holland, remove the stitches and make the incision a bit bigger."

"Wait, why bigger? I don't want to make it worse." Holland deliberated and searched frenziedly between Lena and I.

"Well, it will be easier to move around the camera if the hole is bigger. It's okay. We can stitch it back because it might bother her. Also, let's brace ourselves. She could explode like our last friend." Gabe chuckled under his breath and reminded Holland and I that it was a joke when neither of us laughed. The last person who exploded had the cure and not just Dermadecatis like Lena. "Everyone ready now?" Gabe looked to me for approval, forgetting his sick joke, and I just gaped back unable to move.

Holland observed me for approval since Gabe didn't give the okay. I shrugged because I wasn't ready. I didn't want Lena to change, but I didn't want to hurt her either. This outweighed anything; her hurting or being in pain, I couldn't bear it.

Holland took the stitches out with ease and made an incision, but Lena didn't bleed like a normal body would. Instead, the blood was black and chunks of skin seemed to come off as the cut got longer. Holland's eyes began to water from the smell erupting from Lena's skin. I began to breathe from my mouth, because I didn't want to be grossed out, especially by someone I cared deeply about. Even if it was a few days, I wanted to be with her. I wanted to stop it right then, but I knew we could be saving her life right now. Or could be making it worse. Lena wasn't conscious, but I wondered if she knew we were working on her.

I looked down to her forehead and saw that there were flaps to the opening in her head. Her skin lay opened with dried up black blood coming out. Gabe didn't seem to be repulsed, but I knew Holland was, because she continued to cough into her arm while covering her mouth after she placed the camera carefully into Lena's head.

"Let me take over," I told her quietly. She acted as if she didn't hear me, probably out of pride. "Holland, it's okay. I can take it from here. We'll just swap jobs."

"I was going to be a nurse. I can handle this," she said without moving.

"You weren't going to have to deal with this I am sure. It's okay. Switch," I said once more.

She didn't look sure, but she moved out of the way, and I began to insert more wire into Lena's head. "Okay," Gabe told me slowly. "Steady. Don't want to do anymore damage than is already done."

I moved with extra care as I inserted the wire now, and it wasn't as easy as it looked when Holland did it. The cord was incredibly thin, and guiding it inside Lena's head was hard, because I didn't know where to move the wire. My only guidance was by watching the screen with the camera on it, and even then I had to watch her head at the same time. I kept peeking between the two, but it was difficult. I steadied myself and was surprised at how calm I felt. My focus was making her better. I watched her face to make sure she was out of it and couldn't feel any pain from this. I didn't survey it going into her head anymore, because her face was so beautiful, even now. She was expressionless, and she looked peaceful still. I didn't want to see how much went in, so I continued to watch her face as I pushed the cord little by little. Finally, I turned to the screen to make sure I was going in the right direction. Gabe moved slowly away and left me to keep putting it in deeper.

"Stop," Gabe barked loudly, making me jump. I saw from the corner of my eye that Lena was stirring. Her eyes began to flicker, but she stopped suddenly. I hesitated, but Gabe gave me thumbs-up, and I continued to move the wire down.

Holland walked forward from her job of holding the wire at the right angle. "I'm ready to continue now. I had to just collect myself." When I didn't move, she continued calmly but sternly. "Move, Jared. Now. I want to do this." I moved out of the way, but made sure she had a tight grip on the wire before releasing it.

As Gabe observed the screen for a while, he said, "I'm disappointed. All we can see is darkness. I don't think we'll be able to find the red dot like I suspected. Jared, I'm glad Holland has it now, because we have no idea where to go. So now we can blame Holland when we mess up." Holland didn't look up but scowled.

"Maybe the rotting is deeper than we thought," Holland suggested as I looked to the screen and came to the conclusion that nowhere in her brain looked healthy anymore. That wasn't the worst part; we couldn't find the target area due to so much darkness, thus we wouldn't be able to help her.

"They didn't attack the occipital lobe or the parietal lobe. But the frontal lobe is completely destroyed. She has her memories still, but what has changed then?" Holland asked no one. "I don't see a difference in her. Have you noticed a difference?" she asked me directly this time.

"None. She is the same person as before. I haven't noticed her acting strangely either." I stopped myself. "But I didn't know her that well before either. Just from class." I felt silly, because I felt as if I knew her for so long. Holland looked at me with understanding eyes.

"What's the plan of action?" Holland tested Gabe.

"We'll try to shock out the blackness in there. It's rotted, and I think it's beyond being saved." He went straight to the truth, always. No ounce of hope and no apologies. He didn't meet my eyes. He had no control of what happened to her.

"We have to try. For Jared," Holland voiced to Gabe. Gabe shook his head in agreement, but I could tell he didn't completely agree.

"I'm sorry, Jared. I mean that. I want her to be okay. For you." I gawked back at Gabe in amazement and nodded slowly. Gabe gave a weak smile and strode to the computer again. "Holland, hold her down just in case she jumps a little." Holland braced herself and held Lena down. Gabe hit a button, and I watched the screen. I didn't want to see if it hurt Lena. I would rather be in oblivion.

The screen lit up all around as soon as he hit the button. The blackness returned and Gabe hit the button for a third time, but this time, Lena reacted. And not how we expected.

Lena screamed. It was a loud shrill of a scream. It made my ears feel as if they were bleeding. She opened her eyes and screeched even louder than before. She shrieked as they had rolled to the back of her head, and I was far from calm.

"Lena, look at me. Everything is okay." Holland had backed away, leaving me alone by her side. She didn't even want to look at what she had done. I beheld Gabe and his head was in his hands.

Then I was screaming, "What's wrong? What happened?" No one responded so I searched the screen. Lena's brain was pulsing. I regarded her and saw her head moved in weird waves and directions. I began to yank out the wire. Lena began to convulse and throw up black smelly vomit.

"Do something!" I shouted to Holland while she was screaming some odd prayer. Gabe continued his position, and I halted in place while Lena made a snarling sound. She turned slowly, and I saw that the whites of her eyes were black now. I started to shout and closed my eyes for a second to make sure I wasn't dreaming. Gabe ran forward and yanked the remaining bit of wire out, along with the camera, finishing my previous job. Lena returned lying down and her eyes closed. She was silent. I put my head to her chest and felt her breathing. I turned my face into her, where no one could see me.

In my mind, I was slowly attempting to pull myself together. Holland touched my arm, but I didn't budge. Then Holland pinched me as a sob erupted from her, so I brought my head up. The wires along with the camera were steaming. Lena stirred, and her eyes crept open.

"What happened?" a soft voice asked. She looked sleepy, and I touched her cheek in silence.

The wires along with the camera were singed beyond repair, and it had come from Lena's brain.

Chapter Seventeen: No Clue

AFTER THAT DAY, I didn't let Gabe touch her. After he used thirteen stitches vertically to close the cut, I grabbed her into my arms and carried her upstairs, leaving Holland to clean up the mess. Not that I was mad at Gabe or Holland, but I just didn't trust them with her anymore. Three days had passed, and if Holland were alone with Lena, I would check on her constantly. I was afraid they would try something new without asking her or me.

Lena probably could see that I didn't look at her the same way. I was terrified for her. She was dying, and there was nothing to do but watch. Holland continued to plead with me to just try to help her by going back into her head, but I refused to let them. They didn't want to hurt her, but they had unintentionally. I was haunted by her screams, and I hadn't slept in three days. I couldn't forgive them for not testing their theory out before they worked on her.

She didn't look as happy or uplifting as before, and I couldn't help but feel sad whenever I saw her. She cooked breakfast every morning, and went to hide in her room every afternoon. She only communicated with Holland. I knew I had to talk to her, but I didn't know what to say.

My mind was clouded by demons, and I couldn't get away from them. My father had successfully ruined my life, and I had let him. I wasn't going to let him ruin her soul. He could take her mind or make her rot, but he wouldn't change who she was. I wasn't going to let him.

***

I walked to her room and knocked, but she didn't answer. I opened the door. Lena was on her back across her bed. She had a book up to her face as she laid in her sweatpants. I smiled to her, and she looked up embarrassed.

We didn't speak for a while, and I let the silence transcend through my body. I felt heat run through me, because the way she looked at me was a way that no one else had before. She looked away, breaking the connection, and I gazed down timidly. I was not shy, but she made me that way. She finally spoke to me after a moment of more silence.

"Where have you been lately?" she asked warily. She sat up while crossing her legs and patted the bed for me to sit down. I sat beside her, feeling inferior all of a sudden. "I mean, I guess I wouldn't want to be around me either." She punched me in the arm in a playful way.

"You're so weak, little girl." I smiled, because I used to mean this in an unkind way, now I teased her, but she wasn't weak at all. "I thought you'd want to be alone, I guess."

"Why would I want to be alone? I really need and want company all the time."

"I didn't know. I'll work on that." Her face was frustrated. She saw me staring and grinned a little.

"Good. So, I was wondering if we could play a game." I laughed, and she looked embarrassed. "I mean, the question game. I never got a chance to ask more things. I got sick, if you remember."

How could I forget the day I found out about her being sick? I couldn't believe that I missed all the signs. She was so distant, and I didn't think anything of it. She was so much like her father; he never let anyone know if there was anything wrong. She had a quick mind, and made me feel as if I could do anything with her help. I wanted to make her even better than she was, because she made me better than I was. If she wanted to know the truth about me, then I was going to tell her."Well, what do you want to know?" I asked, testing.

"I want to know what your life was like before this. I want to know how you felt when you first saw me. I can remember that day so clearly," she added.

I hesitated, and she closed her book and sat up for good measure to show me that she was ready to listen. Her face was full of excitement and wonder so I smiled and started. "My life before was full of heartbreak and I wasn't a happy guy. My father was a monster, and I couldn't bear to be near him anymore. I met your father by mistake. He had come over to the house to discuss their project, and I was a nosey kid. I used to sit by the door and listen to my dad's meetings. It was forbidden, and my mother used to spank me if she found me, but I never stopped. I never stopped believing he was evil, and I was right. Your father and mine got into a heated argument. I didn't understand what it was about, so I lingered by the door, and your father nearly knocked me over when he threw it open. I started to run, and he caught up to me. He was so gentle, but I was afraid of him, because I thought he was just like my father. He told me to meet him later that night, which I thought was odd, but he said if I wanted to know the truth, I would have to trust him. I was fifteen then. Your dad saw a strength in me that I didn't know I had." I paused.

Lena's eyes looked glassy and distant. She missed her father. "He didn't tell me about you until I was about seventeen. He didn't tell me, because he didn't know if he could trust me yet with you. He told me that if he ever were to pass that I had to promise to protect you. I was supposed to protect you, and I didn't." My voice broke, but she held me in a tight hug. She was the one who needed comforting, yet there she was giving it to me.

"It's okay," she said soothingly to me. "Keep telling me more."

I paused for a second as I caught my breath but continued. "Your father created the disease itself about four years ago. He thought if he could cure such a deadly disease that the cure for cancer would follow. He created a cure for Dermadecatis after my father stole it from him. My father started giving the disease to people. We tried to find out how he gave it to them, but we didn't know. Your father had the disease locked away in a vile in his lab, but my father found a way past the layers of the lab. Your father went out and died before he could start giving the cure to people. He told me he created the true cure and the answer lies in you. The cure my father created was something far worse than what we anticipated. Your father just thought he would give the disease to the entire world, and that it was up to me to stop it from happening. Your father expected a lot of me. He expected to cure cancer and give the cure to the poor first and then the rest of the world. He was a good man. He didn't want to harm people. He didn't make the disease to hurt people. He thought they would never see Dermadecatis. My father wanted to kill, and I thought that was all. But he really wanted to destroy the human's will to live with the disease and then control human beings with his cure. I didn't think it would ever get this far. He's won, and there is nothing we can do about it."

"Wait." She sat up straighter and in confusion. "My father created the disease? Did I hear that right? My father made strands of disease. Not Dermadecatis. That can't be true." She paused. So she did know things he could do at least.

I waited. I knew she didn't want to think that someone used his disease for something bad. "He didn't create it for evil or to kill people." She looked sad, so I continued. "Don't think badly of your father. My father destroyed his dream of curing cancer and all other forms of disease. My father began spreading the disease, and I had no idea how they spread it until now. Until you."

"Then I won't die in vain. I helped you discover how it was spread." She smiled, and I felt my face fall, but she continued. "Where is the cure?" she asked slowly.

"I really don't know. He never told me. All he ever said to me was 'Lena has the cure. It is in her control,'" I told her in honesty.

Her face transformed to puzzlement, then quickly to awe. "My father said that to me often too. I don't know how, though." She couldn't focus, and I realized she may have the cure, but she had no clue where to find it. "Will you tell me something?" she asked quietly for my ears only.

"Yes. Anything," I said.

"How was your father a monster?" she asked curiously, and I immediately wanted to evaporate. I didn't want to go down that road, but I would tell her.

"Where do I begin?" I hesitated, and she waited thoughtfully. "Your father invented this disease. Not to harm anyone, but to find a cure to end all forms of disease, especially cancer." I reminded her because I didn't want her to forget that he was good. "My father told him it wasn't a good idea, because what would kill us then? We would have to kill each other. Your father said it would be better if everyone died peacefully and in his or her sleep. What a beautiful thought." She smiled, because she knew her father was noble, and I was glad I could give her that much. "So your father tested the disease along with the cure. He inserted the disease into the brain, the heart or the arm of an animal. He started on squirrels." She made a face, and I couldn't help but laugh. "Oh yes. Not the squirrels," I mocked her, and she nudged me to continue. "Well, my father didn't think that animal testing was valuable. So he started to try it on humans. He got many people who were dying already from the hospital, and he inserted them with the disease. They died immediately and were not pronounced dead because of Dermadecatis either. He got a sick pleasure of seeing people so sick and dying. Your father hid away the true cure, and he hid it where no one would find it, except for you. You're meant to find it. But my father invented his own type of cure, and it's to control all those who are sick. He is going to control the entire world if we don't find the real cure."

"And it is ultimately up to me?" She was barely audible, but I nodded.

"It is you who can save us." She let that sink in, and I remained silent for her to collect her thoughts. I rubbed her head, and she seemed to feel content, because she laid it on my lap. I broke through the silence. "Do you miss him?" She lifted her head to see my face. "Your father? Your mother, too."

"Of course. All the time." She smiled. "I have more memories of my mother." Her face turned into disgust. "My father was too busy, and I was so infuriated with him, but now I know why." She looked around the room.

"What is your favorite memory?" I asked, trying to distract her.

"My mother took care of me, no matter what. I used to sit on the roof every day at night to watch the sky. I had a telescope at one point, but it fell off one afternoon when I forgot to take it inside. My favorite memory of her is when I was on the rooftop. I had been crying because my father told me that I wouldn't be able to go outside to my favorite place anymore. He told me that we would get sick. He didn't tell me why. Isaac was sick a week later, though, so I was thankful, but my memory is of my mother. She came onto the top of the house with me. She never went with me on the roof. She let me cry on her shoulder and told me stories of how she met my father. I had never heard that story before. We talked for three hours. She told me she wanted me to enjoy my last time up there, and I was happy because I got to spend it with her." She stopped and took a deep breath to remain calm. "You know, even when she was sick, she was still happy. She would make my favorite food and still went out to buy me books to read, and when she couldn't do things anymore, I made her food like she had my whole life. I watched her cooking, so I knew how. I miss her every day of my life. I want to live for her. I want to make her proud of me." She gasped as her voice caught. I waited for her to continue and rubbed her head again.

"My father is a little different. He wasn't cold, but he didn't love like she did. Or he didn't make it known as she did. I knew he loved me, though, and I loved him, too. He didn't have time for me like she did. He was a busy man, and I really see that now. We rarely had good moments. We didn't fight, but I didn't get along with him, either. When my mother was dying, and when I needed him the most, he was too busy for me. I feel like an idiot now, because I know he was trying to find a cure for her. He was trying to find a cure for everyone, and I was selfish. I wanted his attention. I just thought whenever my mother died that I would have him. It turns out I didn't have either." She didn't cry, and I didn't know how she held it in. I looked to her face and found the struggle of holding in her tears.

"Why did he do this?" she asked to me. I shrugged, but she continued. "So many people have died. My mother." She spoke in broken sobs. "He didn't even have the cure."

I cut her off gently. "Just stop and relax," I told her in a soothing voice. She slowly released another breath and closed her eyes. I wished she knew the cure and how to save the world, but I realized in this moment, she needed someone to save her.

Chapter Eighteen: Isaac

SHE CONTAINED HER composure for what seemed like a long time. I didn't know what to say so I just rubbed her hands in mine. She seemed a little calmer when she finally spoke up to change the subject. "Tell me what you thought when you saw me then." I didn't know if I should talk, but I needed to distract her and make her feel happy.

"First, thank you for telling me things that are personal to you." She bobbed her head, and I continued. "I thought you were amazing. I didn't know it was you. I had no clue that you were the one he always talked about. Your father, I mean. I couldn't even control my feelings when I heard your name in class. I was never in that class for more than a day, so I had no clue that you were in the class. But then your father sent me away, and I came to finish building the rest of this." I threw my hand up to show I meant the safe house.

She looked at me with wonder. "So, this disease has been building up for years. Why didn't my father tell me or warn me about what caused the outbreaks? He could have told me where it was going to be coming from," she said defiantly. Hurt registered all over her face, and I could tell she felt as if he betrayed her.

"Your father never meant for his creation to go amuck. He didn't want to frighten you, to think he created this to harm others. My father wanted to harm the others, not yours."

"How do you know all of this?" she probed calmly. "I wish I could have figured it out before I went to the hospital. They were so odd there."

"I didn't realize it was done in hospitals. You have to believe me. I honestly believed he was abducting people and giving them the disease. That is how it seemed at the square when there was a missing toll instead of a death toll. I couldn't have dreamt up that the hospital was in on this. Unless they are being controlled by my father as we speak." I reached for her face. "I know we can fix this. We'll do everything we can to help you." She looked away, and I felt terrible. This was entirely my fault. I should have read the signs instead of letting her go into that hospital.

"I should tell you what happened after your dad told me the truth." She nodded so I continued. "Gabe, Holland and I had another friend. His name was Isaac. When I say Isaac, I mean the first to die from the disease."

"Isaac Liams," she stated confidently, and I felt a twinge of pain in my stomach that I tried to ignore.

"Yes. Well, I didn't believe your father for a while, but I did eventually, and this only reinforced it. I thought he wanted to get revenge on my dad and get him arrested. Which is ridiculous, but I didn't know what to make of it. My father had never wronged me personally, and I still didn't want to believe that he was a corrupt man. So I went on with life and didn't take your father's advice. Anyway, one day Isaac was with his mom and got into a car accident. He got banged up pretty badly and had surgery on his leg. When he got home, he was fine. He was in perfect shape. He lived next door, so I checked on him a lot. My father was his doctor and would go to check on him daily. Well, one day he called me over because he felt like something was going wrong with his leg and believed he needed the hospital. So, I went over there and took him to the hospital. My father took off his cast, and he was rotting. I should have realized then that the hospital gave it to him, but I was foolish." I looked away in disgust, because I had been so oblivious to the truth "His leg was almost completely gone, so the doctor had to take it off. We dealt with that in our own way, and Isaac was still in good spirits, but I wasn't. Your father warned me of the disease, and I carelessly let one of my best friends get it. I didn't know how, and I didn't know where it came from. All I know is the day after his leg was amputated, it spread to his heart, and he was gone. Isaac was dead, and I blamed myself. After Holland and I escaped the library, I went to my dad and asked him what was going on. He only smiled and said it was time for me to open my eyes and choose a side. I tried to warn my brother, but I didn't get to him in time. He was killed shortly after. I got a phone call while I was building the safe house. I was told many times he died in his sleep, but I knew better." I felt sick, thinking of my brother. He had decided to be with my father and was killed anyway. I didn't care to talk about him, though.

She sat a while, processing what I said. She looked afraid. She cowered under my gaze. "I hid like a coward after your parents died." She winced, but I continued. "Now I know that I have to fight for this to be over and then you came along and got hurt. I came back to town to watch the presentation, because I heard of the cure on the radio with Holland. I saw you in the crowd. I knew I had to talk to you, just one more time before I walked into a death trap. You held me in place, and I knew I should take care of you like I promised before. I wanted to protect you, and I haven't, but I want to make this better. Not out of guilt, but because I love you."

She stopped fidgeting. "Wait, what?"

I had said something wrong and my face burned. She should have had time to think about it or say it first before I thrust it on her. She wasn't ready to say it back, and I knew it.

Then her lips were on mine, not slow, but passionate and fierce. Her hands were in my hair, and I put mine on the small of her back. She was mine, and although she didn't say she loved me, I felt it through her kiss. We wrapped around each other, and I felt whole for that moment. I didn't feel empty like I had since my dad betrayed me.

She pulled away while blushing. "I'm sorry," she said quickly and kissed me again gently. "I love you, too."

"Always," I said to her, and I meant it. Even if she didn't make it, I would always love her and the short time we had together.

Chapter Nineteen: Why Is Everyone Hiding Something?

LENA HAD BEEN missing all day. I didn't think much of it at first, because she had been feeling drowsy the day before, but I figured she would want to talk or show her face at the very least. She didn't seem as if she wanted to be around anyone. Holland had been disappearing in and out of my sight all day, too, so it didn't surprise me when I saw her striding by, giving me a mischievous smile.

"What?" I asked, bored.

"Oh, nothing." She was hiding something. She was always hiding things. She called them surprises. I just called them lies. She laughed, and Gabe passed with his head buried in his iPad. I greeted him, but he just waved me off. This wasn't how days normally went. Normally, Holland was cooking or Gabe was watching TV or down in his lab.

I had been watching movies all day, which seemed like an old practice now. There were more important things to do, but I didn't know how to make Lena feel better. I didn't know if she wanted to be left alone today, because she felt bad. I let her have her space, because she might need to think about what I said last night.

Holland cleared her throat. "I wanted to ask you something." She didn't look past me like she normally did when Gabe was in the room, so it was serious. She often stared at him in annoyance or in awe.

"What's up?" I asked as she sat beside me. She moved her strawberry-blonde hair to the side and grinned again the same way.

"What was the plan when you left for our hometown?" She looked at me suspiciously, and I didn't say anything. I turned away, and she slammed her hand down onto my leg.

"What did I tell you? You didn't have the strength to do it, and there's nothing wrong with that. Next time, I vote I do it. It's no big deal." She looked at me with innocence.

I stared bewildered at her. How could she say I didn't have the strength? "First of all," I said defensively and a little annoyed, "I didn't kill him because how was I supposed to do it in front of everyone who trusts him? He has followers, you know? The newscast was there. I would have been a wanted man. Even more wanted than I am right now. I would have been killed, and that was something we didn't think of." She began to speak, but I put my hand up to silence her. "Second, I saw her." I didn't continue with this explanation. She shook her head in silence. She got it, and I knew why she got it.

"You knew you would be killed before you left," she said slowly. "But then you saw her and everything changed. I know. I'm sorry to be so selfish." She looked ashamed of what she said. It dawned on me that she truly understood where Gabe didn't.

"It's okay. Don't beat yourself up. I'm sure Gabe put this in your head." All she did was nod, and I couldn't help but feel the anger build up. Gabe wanted this over, so he could go out into the world unharmed. He was a coward sometimes, though. If he had so much to say, he could have told me already.

"Don't beat Gabe up about it. He loves you. He's just cold and indifferent now." There she went, making excuses for Gabe as she always did.

I didn't know what happened between Gabe and I, but a wedge had been between us since my return. I wasn't supposed to return, and they both knew it. It was because I didn't sacrifice myself for him. The truth is, I didn't sacrifice myself for anyone, which was selfish. I didn't sacrifice myself for Gabe, Holland and the rest of the world. But neither Gabe nor Holland wanted to do the deed either.

"I guess I won't," I explained calmly. "I would beat you up, but I don't hit girls." She smiled gently. After a second, a giggle spilled from her lips. After a moment, I was laughing with her.

Holland stood and reached for my hand. "I want to show you something." I hesitated but grabbed it. She sprinted while pulling me behind her. We entered the library, and I was in astonishment. The chandelier was lit and its glow made the books look alight with flames. In the center of the room, there was a circular table sat. There were two spaces set up around it. Holland waited for me to say something as I looked around.

"What is this?" I asked her in amazement. And then it hit me. "No, you didn't," I said with a chuckle and shook my head.

"Well, I think you'll agree that you and Lena haven't had a formal date yet. I would like to blame the disease, but I blame you." She smirked at me as I flicked her off. "Hey now, I can take this down. I'm doing this for her more than you. She wants a date. I know she does. She wants to see you in action. You have never even dated anyone else. And she was the girl you always spoke of, so now I'm giving you a date."

"Thank you," was all I could manage to say. My throat constricted with emotion.

"You're welcome." She smiled. I owed her. It was beautiful, and Lena would love it.

"Is there anything I can do?" I asked.

"Go get dressed. You should look super nice. I'm cooking. Gabe said he would help, but you know how that goes." She shrugged. "He's going to watch the food. I'm going to get Lena up. She's slept all day, bless her heart."

I looked down. That was why Lena had been avoiding me all day. She had been sleeping, and I was immediately scared. Lena was getting worse, and who knew how long she would have. The thought scared me and a pain spread through my body. I couldn't handle losing her.

"Go get ready, silly," she told me, and I walked to my room. What do people wear on dates? I had no clue. I had never gone on a date before in my entire life. Unless you counted the time when Gabe got me a double date, which ended disastrously. Gabe, being Gabe, had offended his date. Lena was the first girl I had ever told that I loved, and I didn't know where to begin with a date. My palms began to sweat, and I had to sit down. I sat and looked around. I was startled when I heard rustling behind me.

Holland walked into the room with clothes in her hand. "I might be a little too pushy, so I'm sorry," she said apologetically. "But I brought you some clothes. You don't have to wear them. Seriously, just a suggestion." She laid the clothes on the back of my desk chair and backed away. "Just a suggestion," she reassured me.

She closed the door, and I walked to the desk. She had picked out khaki pants and a nice polo shirt. I smiled, because deciding something decent to wear was out of the question. Now all I had to think about was what to say and what to do.

Lena had never made me feel nervous. Loving her was as easy as breathing, and I couldn't let her know I was nervous. I started to pace like Gabe did when his nerves took over.

What if she didn't like the nervous me? I wondered if she was even up for a date. Could she even keep down food? Every time we ate, she got sick or felt worse. I felt useless. I couldn't help her the way I wanted to help her.

Then a voice in my mind spoke. *What is wrong with you? Just be yourself.* And then I knew what I had to do. Be me.

***

I had been ready for what felt like an eternity. It turned out it had been only an hour, which was practically the same thing to me. I sat and watched TV while Gabe ignored me as he typed on his iPad. I wanted to talk to him, but he was being so odd.

"Gabe," I said quietly, and he looked up at once. Maybe he could hear the defeat in my voice. "Is everything okay?"

"Yeah. I just have been thinking of ways to help Lena today. I don't know what there is to do." He turned the screen to me. And I saw the image of a brain that was deformed and immediately realized whose it was. "I made a sketch of how her brain looks. I was trying to remember what happens when each lobe of the brain is damaged. Each damage is equally bad."

He didn't explain what he meant, and I was grateful that he wasn't being blunt. I didn't know if I could take it. "So what's the solution?"

Gabe didn't turn to me and he spoke to the couch. "Jared, it seems that she'll die if we don't hand her over." He didn't look at me, but heard the hopelessness in his voice.

"No," I yelled to him. "We haven't tried everything. We've only tried one thing. I know I told you not to touch her again, but if it is necessary, then you must help," I shouted over the TV.

He flinched but didn't back down, and he faced me. "Jared, do you want her dead or alive as a different person?" There was the bluntness I didn't want.

I didn't answer, because neither option sounded like something I could live with. "Neither. Can't we just try something new?" I pleaded calmly.

"Enjoy your night, and we can discuss this in the morning. We can try one of my theories, but what if they damage something in her brain? Think about that."

"I would still love her and want to be with her," I told him, and his face softened.

"Enjoy tonight. You need to be with her and show her how much she means to you." He got up, and I got the feeling there was something he wasn't telling me.

Chapter Twenty: First Dates, Last Dates

I WAITED IN the kitchen alone for Lena while Gabe was downstairs in the lab, completely ignoring his duty of watching the food. So I made it my job to make sure nothing burnt. I continued to wait for about forty more minutes, and I slumped in my seat with annoyance. I wanted to ask him why he was still looking when he had no intention of helping Lena, but I decided against it. I didn't want to fight with him. I heard a door slam, and I walked to the hallway and saw Gabe with his nose in his iPad again.

"What's wrong?" I asked angrily. "Shouldn't you be watching the food?" I could tell he was embarrassed because he slouched over as he walked into the kitchen and rested a hand on his face. He had every reason to be. He didn't want to help her, and he should have been ashamed.

"Why should we both be up here while you're watching?" he asked sarcastically before continuing. "Jared. I want to help her. I don't want to just let something bad happen to her. I'm panicking at this point. I have no clue what the right thing is to do with her." He didn't seem to be dealing very well with the fact that he had no idea what to do, but he continued. "I know you love her. If I didn't want you happy, I wouldn't be here searching for answers. Maybe I can figure out something. Enjoy your night and let me fix this. I will fix this for you." He put his hand out for me to shake, and I laughed and slapped it away. "I'll watch the food now. I promise." He laughed as he threw his hands up, but something caught his eyes. He froze in place. Holland walked forward, and I wanted to chuckle, because Holland made him shut up. No one made Gabe shut up. Ever.

Then I saw her. Lena wore a tight black skirt that grazed the tops of her thighs with a silky gold shirt that hung loosely on her shoulders. Her shoes were black heels that were high enough to reach my height, and I knew that Holland put her up to it. Then I reached her face and saw why Gabe froze in place. It was her face, perfectly clear with no trace of rotting skin in sight. Holland must have covered it with makeup. Her eyes looked glassy but stunning. They were bright green, but her right eye seemed to have dimmed even more than before, but they made my heart soar as she stared at me fiercely through them.

"Sorry we took so long, but I wanted you to feel comfortable." Holland faced Lena. Lena smiled sweetly and pulled Holland into a bear hug. She whispered something, and when Lena released the hug, I saw Holland holding her mouth as tears spilled from her eyes.

"Have fun, you two," Holland barely made out as she backed down the hallway to her room, probably to recover from whatever Lena had said.

Lena walked to me, and it was like a glow was around her. She walked straight into my arms and she didn't have to stand on her tiptoes because of her shoes. She was shorter than me, and it was nice to see her face straight on for once. She wrapped a hand around my neck and pulled me into an embrace. Her lips found mine, and I forgot where I was until Gabe cleared his throat. Lena moved quickly away as she blushed.

"Sorry, Gabe," she told him, but I knew she didn't mean it, because she gave me a look as if to say *later*.

"Shall we?" I asked delicately. She nodded, and I looped my arm through hers as she giggled. It sounded almost natural. It was as if she wasn't sick at all. Maybe she didn't feel sick, because Holland made sure she didn't look sick. I led her down the hallway, and Holland looked out to the hallway from her room. Tears still filled her eyes, and she moved away to the shadow of her room as we passed by.

All the nerves from earlier had swept away as soon as I saw her. I knew who I had to be and what to say whenever she walked into the room. I had to be myself. The person she already cared for and loved. I opened the door to the library, and Lena gasped at the sight. Even now, it was as if I were seeing it for the first time. The light almost glittered into the air. Her eyes glistened with tears, and I wanted to cry as well. I was so glad to be there with her.

"You did this for me?" she asked in amazement just as I did earlier. She grinned for a while, waiting for me to answer. When I hadn't, she chuckled lightly. "It's a test." She beamed at me. I was at a loss for words, and I finally recovered.

"No, I didn't," I said finally and cleared my throat. "Holland set this up, but I hope that's not a problem. I'm just really dumb when it comes to signs, I guess." I smirked as she made a face of shock.

"Ah," she remarked. "I wondered if you'd be honest. Holland already told me that she was the mastermind behind this." The lights hit her eyes and they shimmered radiantly. She looked around the room in admiration. The light flickered, and she rotated to me.

"I love books. When I was younger, I told my parents that I wanted a library for myself, just me. I wanted a chair and a lamp and then all four walls covered with books. Reading is my escape. If I had a bad day, I wanted to read and go to a different world." I watched her in enchantment as she walked along the shelves, brushing her hands along each book as if they were a sea of pages. "I just wanted a room of my own where my imagination would run free. My father promised me he would build it for me one day, but my mom was so sick he focused all his time on finding the cure. I forgave him, and I know that he would have given me the world if he could have. I was such a selfish child." She looked ashamed of herself. "I wanted too much and took too much for granted. I never want to do that again. I want to put others before myself from now on. I want to put you before me. Do what you think is right for me. I'm fine with whatever the outcome as long as you're happy."

I couldn't bear to see the way she talked down on herself, but I stood in place. "That isn't fair. You matter, too. You matter more than I do, because this is your life. You shouldn't have to feel like you can't decide your fate. I want you to tell me what the best thing is for you to do. I will not take away your decision."

She didn't seem convinced. "I think that I will let you and Gabe do whatever you need to while you try to fix me, but if you can't, it's okay. I want you happy, and I'm fighting to hang on, I really am, but I don't know how long I will last."

She looked defeated. I grabbed her into a full embrace. She relaxed from her tense stance as soon as my arms wrapped around her. "Don't talk like that. I won't give up and Gabe won't either, so neither should you." I spoke into her hair and gave her kisses in between each word. She giggled as I tried to tickle her.

"Let's forget this tonight. We can focus on that tomorrow. What do you say?" I extended my hand to her, and she grasped it tightly. I brought her to the table and kissed her hand as I pulled out her chair for her to sit. She smiled and told me "Thank you" as she lowered herself to sit.

"Okay. So what's on the menu for tonight?" she asked eagerly. She nearly jumped in her seat, and I was full with butterflies. This was a side I had never seen from her.

"Holland is making a roast and a surprise dessert." She nodded and didn't say much. I wondered if she was feeling nervous now. As I sat, she wrapped her foot around mine. She smiled widely to me, and I grinned back.

She was happy, and I could almost forget that she was sick. Her face was covered flawlessly. Her blouse was beautiful and on top it was the necklace she always wore. She even slept with hit. I noticed it when we had stayed in the motel. It glowed in the flicker of the lights now. I never asked her why she wore it, and I didn't know if she would tell me. It must be important to her.

My gaze lingered a little too long, because she instantly grabbed it and began to twirl the key in her hands. "It's beautiful," I told her. "Why do you always wear it? Do you just love it that much?"

She looked down as she spoke. "My father gave it to me the day he died. It is my favorite memory of him actually. I loved it when I got it, but now it means much more than that. It was the last thing he gave me. It's very special to me." She didn't look sad; she instead looked angry. I grabbed her chin and lifted it until she was eye level with me.

"What is it? What's wrong? We don't have to talk about anything. I just wondered where it came from," I said in puzzlement.

"I'm just so angry that I didn't see that this would happen. I shouldn't have let my mom go out, and my dad shouldn't have gone out that day. He was hiding, and I fought with him the night before to come and then he died." Angry tears streamed down her face. "Dang it. My makeup will be ruined, and I will have to face the truth."

"Hey," I said softly and got up to kneel beside her. "It's not your fault. He knew what would happen. He knew what was coming. He wanted you safe and you were. He is watching over you and always will."

"Then why did this happen to me?" she asked gingerly.

"This is my fault. I didn't protect you, and I'm sorry. I broke my promise to him to keep you safe. I should have put the clues together. You were losing so much blood that day. I didn't think twice about the hospital." I felt a stab in my heart as I remembered why she was in this situation to begin with.

"It isn't your fault. I would have been dead anyway from blood loss. I could have been looking for a cure myself, but I was selfish and lived in a depression."

"You had every right to feel that way. You lost special people to you. It is okay. Don't cry. We can talk later. We should enjoy our date."

I wiped her eyes and her cheeks. "You're right. Let's have fun." She faked a smile, and I kissed her cheek, then her forehead, and she stifled a chuckle. She kissed my nose and winked to me. As soon as I sat back down, Holland walked in with our food.

"How are the love birds?" she asked in a cheerful tone. "Gabe gave up on me and went to the lab. He never stops." I flinched, but tried to hide how I was feeling right now. Holland continued. "I made something I think you will love for dessert. I'm so excited. I watched the Food Network last night for the recipe." She babbled on, but I just stared at Lena while Lena gazed up at Holland. Holland continued to speak and then when I glanced back up to her, she was gone.

We were silent when Holland left. Until Lena's soft voice broke through. "I wish I had good friends like you do. I mean, my only friend abandoned me the night I saw you." She stopped in place as her head fell between her hands. "What if Kaley died that night?" Her face turned to desolation. "Although you told me she wasn't a good friend, I still worry about her. And you know what's sad? I believe you when you say she talked badly about me. Full heartedly. But what happened to her? I will never know."

"Gabe can find out for you, because we have records on everyone missing from that day. You are wonderful, and who cares if you don't have her as a friend. You made two new friends here." She looked down to her food and picked up her fork.

"I would like to find out what happened to her. You're my friend, too. You're like my best friend." I knew she meant this, and I thought so, too. I loved her much more than a friend, though. That was when a sickness fell over me. I didn't want to be dishonest with her ever. I had to tell her the truth.

"There's something I want to tell you. I want to be honest always." She gripped my hand from across the table. Her grasp was tight to encourage me to go on.

"Lena, I went back home to find my father."

Her face dropped. "So, you lied to me?" she asked quietly.

"Well, yes. I was on a mission to kill him. I was going to shoot him, but then I thought, what logic is that? So many followers have the information already. Gabe tried to tell me this before I left home, but I wanted my own revenge."

"So what?" she asked as hurt registered all over her face.

"I knew I was going to die if I shot him in front of those people. As soon as I saw you, out and about, I knew they would target you. And I didn't want to save you, not at first. I thought you were a silly girl who knew nothing. But then I thought of your father and I remembered you were his world, and I kept replaying how he said the answers lie in you. And I knew that I had to save you or stop them from hurting you." I hesitated and gripped her hand because she had loosened her tight grasp. "Lena, I want you to know that this is real. Your dad didn't make me come find you. I just didn't want you to be afraid of me. I wanted to help the world, and eventually, I wanted to help you."

"Is there more that you've hidden from me?" she whispered. It pierced the silence, and I wished she'd yelled instead.

"No. I." I stopped. There was more. There was no hope of her surviving anymore. Should I tell her? I didn't know what the right thing to do was. So I picked honesty. "Gabe is losing hope after the last time we went into your brain."

"What does that mean?

"It means you might not have much more time with me. We have to make the most of this. I want you forever, and I want to fix you, but what if we can't? I just found a reason to hold on and live, and it's being taken from me."

Tears filled her eyes, and I felt them reaching mine, but I had to be strong for her, for us. I felt like an idiot for ruining our moment, but I wanted to be honest with her. I loved her, and she was strong. She and I both knew she could handle anything.

"I wish I could always be here with you," she said slowly, "but I told myself the truth a while ago, and even if I'm not on earth with you, I'm with you always. I've realized something else that I didn't want to tell you."

"What is that?" I asked quietly after a few seconds, breaking the silence.

"That I really think I'm in love with you. You have protected me this whole time, and brought me to this house. You have made me feel like I understand my father now. Wait, you did know my father, right?" She smirked at me, and I reached across the table and touched her face.

"Well, I do know that I love you. I'm in love with you and I know it. It's okay if you aren't sure if you love me this way. I will always wait for you," I told her.

"We don't have much time to think, though," she stated quietly. "I'm in love with you. Not because the time is gone, but because no time will ever be enough with you. I will love you, and you will always remember in here." She pointed to my heart.

She stood and plopped down onto my lap. For a moment, we forgot our troubles as she kissed me. She put her head against my neck and whispered that she loved me. And for the moment, that was enough.

Chapter Twenty-One: I Don't Want Tonight To Be Over Yet

WE FINISHED THE dinner, and Lena was glowing. She continued to sit on my lap even when we ate the caramel cake that Holland made. We split a piece and then another.

I discovered little things about her that night. I realized stuff she didn't have to tell me. Like the way she scrunched her nose when she talked about something she didn't like or when she was frustrated. She glowed as her laughs echoed off the walls. I couldn't get over what I discovered.

She smiled at me and laughed at my jokes as if they were the funniest things she had ever heard, even when I knew they were terrible. We laughed in our little paradise for six hours. I found out she loved to sing when she sang a song, and we danced to her voice. I fell in love with her even more that night.

She asked me questions that no one else ever cared to ask about. She asked about pets and my favorite memories. She cared about the little things. Then she asked the question I almost wished I never had to answer.

"Do you have any siblings?" She stopped short when my face turned cold. "Oh no. I'm sorry. I remember that you had a brother." She bit her lip.

"I did have a brother." She froze, and I looked away toward the chandelier.

She spoke softly. "If it's not too much to ask, what happened really? You didn't tell me a lot." She looked gloomy, and I was sure it was because my face looked so wretched. She hesitated. "You don't have to, of course." She bit her lip in angst.

After a few moments, I felt myself float back to the time that I last saw him. "His name was Aiden. He was my best friend. My father murdered him," I told her calmly.

"Oh no. I'm so sorry." Her eyes glistened with tears, but I didn't feel sad. I felt angry.

"My father murdered him because he stayed behind when I went to build the safe house. He was younger than me. He didn't want to betray my father and leave him alone. He wanted to be the golden child. That was his curse," I told her. I didn't want to remember the sadness his memories brought me. "He got in the way. I'm surprised he didn't control Aiden's mind. It would have been easier, given how young Aiden was. I'm glad that Aiden died instead of being controlled. I wouldn't want to see him under my dad's rule. I loved him so much." My voice broke, and she hugged me.

She didn't speak for a while. I thought it was because she wanted to give me time. So she held my hand for a long time and kissed my palm a few times. Eventually, she held my gaze so long I couldn't help but feel happy again.

After a while, we went back to my room. She led the way, and she kissed me all the way to the bed. But what was amazing was she didn't once lead me to believe that I would have more than a kiss. And I didn't.

***

I opened my eyes and there she was. She was wearing what she had worn the night before, and I smiled. Suddenly, I felt self-conscious; was she happy to be sleeping there?

I looked down and observed her. She began to stir, and my heart started to pound.

She weakly stared up at me. "Good morning." She smiled and began to get up, but I pulled her down.

She started to laugh and then she gasped. I quickly loosened my grip and she was dashing. I didn't follow quickly behind her, because I knew she was going to get sick. My blissful morning ended sooner than I wanted. I yelled for Holland to come, because I knew Lena still wanted her company.

Holland raced to the bathroom from the kitchen and shut the door behind her. I leaned my head on the wall, and Gabe walked behind me.

"Oooo," he said in a girlish tone. "Did I see her leaving your room?" He smiled at me and winked.

"Okay. Don't ever wink again, creep," I told him, and he sneered.

"Well, tell me. What happened?"

"Nothing. I actually care about her," I retorted calmly, feeling my temper escalating.

"Or you're just stupid. I mean, how much more time do you think you have with her? I would do it as a soon as possible." He winked yet again.

I scowled at him, and I felt my face wrinkling in frustration. "Who says I don't have time with her? You don't know, nor do I, how long it will be. We have to keep fighting and trying. I won't give up. And you know what, Gabe, it's not something you should rush or take so lightly." I shoved past him.

The truth was, I was a nervous wreck, and I didn't know how Lena would feel about that subject. Also it was too soon. Maybe not for me, but for her, and I knew I would have to talk to Holland about this because Gabe was obviously not a candidate. The door opened to the bathroom, and I rushed back. Holland came out wearing a gloomy face.

"What is it?" I asked in a flash.

"She is just getting so much worse. We need to make the most of her right now. I don't know what Gabe and I can do. I will go talk with him. Try to get her to come out if you can."

I moved toward the door, but everything was blurry in my eyes. This just proved that there wasn't much that I could do. I wanted to give her the best last days. I had to decide if she should go to my dad to get the cure or not. She deserved life and happiness. I wasn't sure what her wishes were. I didn't think I could live with myself if she were dead.

"Lena." I knocked on the door lightly. There was no response. "I must really gross you out if you had to run away from me." Then I remembered it was soundproof, so I knocked loudly again.

The door opened slightly and a voice erupted from it. "Will you get my toothbrush?" she asked quietly.

"Sure." I ran down the hallway and into her room. It smelled of lavender, and I felt sick because she made the room feel like her own in a matter of days. She was always herself and she always wanted to be herself, no matter where she was. She was happy and safe with me. I let her down. I let her get sick. I turned away and got her toothbrush from the bathroom sink.

I jogged back to her and knocked. She opened the door, reaching only her hand out. I gave her the toothbrush, and she quickly shut the door. Holland came out of the lab and beckoned me forth while putting a hand over her mouth to tell me to be quiet.

"What?" I demanded as I approached her.

"Gabe wants to call for a meeting, as he said it. So when she is done, come on." She walked away, and I felt uneasy while I waited for Lena.

As I approached the door, it opened and she ran to me. She jumped on me, and I pulled her into my arms. I squeezed her, and her lips found me. She wrapped her arms around me, and I held her head up to mine.

I felt so at ease, but then I remembered. "I hate to break this up, but Gabe is calling a meeting," I told her, and her face fell as she jumped down.

"Let's go." She grabbed my hand, and we walked in silence down to the lab.

Gabe and Holland were both looking down while leaning against the table. It was just like we had found them when we had arrived, but with a new a dilemma and a graver one, in my opinion. When we reached the bottom of the steps, Holland looked up and shared a small smile with Lena.

"What's going on?" Lena asked Holland.

"Gabe," Holland said softly without looking at Lena. I felt apprehensive because of Holland's uneasiness. Gabe stepped forward, looking beyond both our faces.

"I just want to tell you that I want to keep trying. I'm just afraid of the consequences. So we wanted to ask you first." He directed his full attention to her.

"What consequences?" she asked calmly.

"If we were to damage any part of your brain, I don't know how we would fix it. Have you ever heard of Phineas Gage?" he asked.

"I have. The railroad accident correct?"

"The very one." He smiled, because she knew something as well as he did. "The same thing could happen to you. We could destroy something in your brain. We could make you blind. Or we could make you a different person completely. We don't want those risks."

"I'd rather be blind than dead or a piece of rotting meat." She closed her eyes. "Let's get started." I was glad she was willing to risk her life to get better, but I didn't want her to lose herself or her sight or her hearing. Then I had a wonderful thought.

"Wait!" I shouted.

"What?" Everyone turned to me, alerted.

"What if we target her arm first? What if we can see how this heals and then we'll see how to heal her head."

Gabe looked to Holland, and Holland was pouring with enthusiasm. "What could it hurt? Would that work?"

"But what if we were to mess up? What if it made it worse? Why did it spread there to begin with? They injected her in the head and not the arm."

"How do we know that?" Holland inquired to Gabe.

Lena squeezed my hand lightly, and I looked down to her, and she was eyeing all around the room into the distance. "I didn't know I was worth saving like this," she said only where I could hear.

I tilted her chin up so she could see me. "You are worth saving. Don't forget that." She nodded against my hands. She should have known we loved her, and we would fight for her.

"Gabe, we have to try," Holland urged.

"What if we make it spread even more?"

"We could try what you made?" she asked him, and his face contorted.

"Absolutely not. Don't be ridiculous. That could kill her." Gabe looked away in dread. I didn't understand why.

"What could kill her?" I inserted. They both turned, and Holland's face was red from being flustered.

"I made an antidote to the disease. But the thing is, I don't know what could happen if we injected her with it." Gabe proudly held up the antidote. "I conjured this up last night."

"How sure are you about it working?" I had to know that she would be safe.

"About eighty percent. I won't give her it. I really am not."

"Ask Lena," Holland quietly remarked and all pairs of eyes turned to her.

Lena looked indifferently at Gabe and just nodded. "I will try it if all else fails. I want to be better, and you know what? If I get worse, I was going to die anyway." She looked to me as her face scrunched, and I couldn't believe how small I felt and how brave she was.

"Let's try the things that could damage me first and then let's try the antidote," she told us. It was as if she was reassuring herself that she was brave enough.

Chapter Twenty-Two: The Antidote

GABE SEEMED NERVOUS as he tried to blast through her brain again. This time he tried to zap a new place, but the same things happened to Lena. Holland tried to obliterate the disease inside her arm, but the result was the same. The wire came out fizzing again, and she resisted all types of treatments. We all knew we would have to use the antidote.

"Do it," she said calmly and nodded to herself.

She grabbed my hand, and I smiled to her. "I'll be with you the entire time."

"If something bad happens, I love you." I shuddered at her words.

"I love you. Nothing bad is going to happen," I reassured her.

Gabe came slowly to her as he prepared the syringe. "Okay. This is going to burn and sting everywhere. No one will know how bad this hurts so no one will judge you if you scream." No hint of sarcasm was there. I death stared him. "What? I had to warn her."

She laughed, and said, "Bring it on. I won't even scream." She smiled and then said, "Okay. Totally kidding, but bring it on, and thank you for sparing me lies." He looked flattered that someone was appreciative of his ways.

I gripped her hand, and she held tightly as Holland rubbed alcohol on her forehead. "Should we try the arm first?" I felt so nervous and my voice shook fiercely.

"I think it would be better to inject the target area. It's worse here, and she was injected with the disease here. When we tried to zap her arm, there wasn't much to zap. The rotting has spread to so many places, not just her arms but her legs and stomach. She told Holland where they all are. Don't worry. This will work." Gabe nodded sufficiently at me. "Trust me, Jared. I really think this is the antidote."

I put my hand down, and Lena put hers back in mine as Gabe injected her. Then she was screaming. She thrashed about, and Holland held her down and looked from Gabe to me.

"I wish I could make the pain go away," she told us, and I wished I was the one feeling the pain for her, too. I couldn't stand how bad she was feeling.

Lena gasped for air as her eyes rolled into the back of her head.

"When does it stop?" I barely made out. Gabe looked at me and shook his head, because he didn't know.

"Then how long until it works?" I asked him in a shrill.

"It is supposed to start destroying the rotting tissue immediately, but maybe I calculated it wrong. I'm not sure." Gabe looked frantically to his computer, but there were no answers there.

Lena reached for her forehead as tears fell from her eyes. "Kill me," she screamed at the top of her lungs, and Gabe turned away. I thought I saw his eyes glistening. "Please," she screamed, and tears spilled from my eyes.

I pulled her into a tight hug as she began to hit my back. I felt tears falling fresh and hot all over my back from Lena. Then there was silence. I pulled back and looked at her face. Slowly, the dark from her forehead was disappearing. Skin seemed to be growing over the gaping hole that was once there. She gently lifted her hand to her head, and she began to laugh. It made no sense, but all at once, my heart started beating again and a warm feeling came over me.

"Lena," I said calmly. "It's going away." She laughed, and I brought her lips to mine. We stayed this way until Holland touched my shoulders.

"You can save that for later. I need to check her blood content and make sure she really is cured." She turned to Gabe. "You're a genius. You're amazing." She smiled at him, and I smiled at him. He looked down, almost ashamed, and I was uncertain why. I kissed Lena and backed away. I watched over her as Holland checked everything.

She looked so healthy. She looked as if she were glowing instead of turning black all over like before. I felt myself ease up, and I turned to look to Gabe, to tell him thank you, but he had left the room.

Chapter Twenty-Three: The Side Effect

LENA AND I were happy as ever that day. She braided her hair in fancy ways all around her head.

"Your hair is beautiful," I told her as she beamed at me.

"If I had a normal life, I would be a hairdresser," she told me. "I would have gone to school with Kaley, but now that I know that Kaley isn't really my friend, I'm thankful I didn't." She paused but continued beaming at me. "I'm glad things are this way instead. I wanted a simple life, but my father had mixed it up whenever he had to do things for his work. I didn't hate that he was a doctor, just the things he missed in my life."

"He missed things for the right reason. Don't forget that," I told her.

"He missed my dance competitions and recitals. He missed out when I rode my first bike, and I was sad over it. I never blamed him, just his job." She looked down sadly. "I'm so happy he left me with the job to save people. That is my gift. Isn't it? My true meaning." She smiled, and I felt content.

Lena cooked me blueberry cobbler, which was my favorite when my mother used to make it. I hated to admit it, but Lena made it better.

Lena told me about her life before Dermadecatis. She told me how her mother got the disease and how her father's light left his eyes as she got sicker. She was glad they got to die together and one didn't have to suffer over the other.

Lena was so selfless, and it made me love her even more. We could learn each other slowly and happily. I loved her, and I knew she loved me. We didn't have to rush anymore. Not the intimate parts, not the dates, not anything. Not anymore. We could grow old together if we wanted to. We could hide out there forever.

As if she read my mind, she asked, "How can we help the people out there, Jared?" I snapped back to reality. We had to help them. We had the medicine to help them, and I knew we would have to do that. She wanted to always be there for others, and I was glad she had this quality, but she was finally fixed.

"We'll figure something out," I told her. "But let me enjoy you being safe."

She smiled at me and kissed me. She dragged me down to the bed, and we kissed for a while and fell asleep. It was complete bliss that she was happy and healthy again. I loved her.

***

In my dream someone stood over me in the darkness. They moved swiftly across the room. When I opened my eyes, there was only blackness. I looked beside me, and Lena was there still. In the dark room, she didn't look well, but she was. It was just my imagination, because I wasn't used to her being better. I felt her face and it was clammy so I got up to open the door to let some air inside. As I was up, I went out to get water in the kitchen, but stopped in the hallway when I saw that Gabe was there. He never seemed to sleep anymore.

He looked surprised to see me. "Can we talk?" he asked softly when he saw I was up.

"What's up man?" I asked quietly.

"I hate to do this." He hesitated, and I panicked.

"Oh no. What is it? Did she not get cured for real?" Panic was all in my voice. I didn't calm down until he said that's not what it was about. "What is it then?" I whispered wildly into the darkness. He led me to the kitchen and turned to me sharply.

"I have discovered something. I didn't want to tell you, but I wanted to try it out first."

"What is this? What is going on? You're freaking me out," I said as calmly as I could when all I felt was complete dread.

"She is not who she says she is. What I put in her was actually a dye deactivator," he said and hung his head down.

"I don't... I don't understand," I said calmly.

"She works for your father, Jared." The world collapsed, and I looked from him to the darkness of my room where she was lying, sleeping.

"How do you know that?" I asked defensively.

"Look at this." He handed me a set of papers. It was the call log from Lena's room. Gabe did get all of the bills for all the things that worked in the house, including the phones.

"Recognize that number? That's your father's." He handed me the records.

A sick feeling passed over me. This was his number. This was the number of the man who betrayed me, and there was unease in the pit of my stomach that made me feel wrong at the moment. I didn't think this was real, but I didn't know what to feel. "She was never sick, Jared. She was faking it the whole time. The dye made the black go away," he told me again.

"Explain the hole in her head. Explain the smell coming from her body? Explain the sickness that

Holland saw. Explain the wires that came out of her head completely singed. Explain it all," I said in shock.

He didn't speak, but instead glared at me in anger. "Don't be stupid," he said.

He didn't look sad, so I tried to defend her one last time. "You're lying."

"Go ask her. Go ask Holland." He didn't face me still.

"She said she saw things. I heard her. She said she felt lumps. She said all those things," I half- whispered, half-shouted to him.

"She saw nothing, and that is what we were searching for. Why she was hiding everything."

"You know what? You're angry because I have someone and you have no one. I know what this is about," I said defiantly.

And then he was laughing. "Yes, I'm jealous of a girl working to destroy you. She almost did. You have never been so wrapped around someone. She is using you. She is luring you in to bring you to your father. I'm right, and you know it." He didn't smirk, he just stared me in the eyes as if he was claiming to be the person who was right and I was the idiot who believed her.

I didn't believe him, and I was infuriated. I snatched the papers from his hands and I stormed down the hall and into my room. I smacked the lights on, and I walked to her. She was waking up slowly. She was smiling at me until she saw my face, and she cowered down like she knew what was wrong already.

I threw the paper down onto her bed. "Explain this. Now," I shouted in her face.

"What? What is that?" she asked as she gathered the paper and a blank expression came over her.

"This is your phone record," I said in an urgent tone.

I had the sick urge to hit something, but I didn't. I focused on her soft eyes. She grabbed the papers and looked taken aback. "This is from my room? I haven't called anyone. I don't have anyone to talk to out there." She pointed to the walls. I saw her eyes are glassed over as if she couldn't believe it.

"Do you know whose number that is?" I asked through gritted teeth.

"Well, it is familiar, but I don't know. I think they used to call my house for my father. But why does that matter?" she shouted.

"That is my father's number, and your room has called him over twenty times." Her face grew from curiosity to confusion.

"I don't know what you're talking about. I have nothing to say to him. He killed my family. Don't you remember? Don't be stupid." She tossed the paper back to me, and I felt my blood boil.

"You work for him, don't you?" The fury I felt spilled over and the shock on her face pushed me over the edge. "You do! You can't even answer me."

"I just thought you knew me better than that," she said simply as she laid her head back down.

"You weren't even sick. Gabe put dye remover in you to see if you were faking, and take a look at you now. You're all cured and not rotting anymore. You are a liar. And I suggest you leave before I kill you. You betrayed me, and you betrayed my friends. I was a mess and worried sick over a liar. You made me care for you. You should leave now."

She just stared at me. There was no remorse in her eyes. I felt my anger faltering, but then she stared at me. "Yes, you are an idiot." My mouth dropped open when she walked past me to her room. "I'll leave in the morning, but you should know that you're wrong, and you lost the person who would have given you everything. I would never side with someone who betrayed you and me in different ways. I'll be gone tomorrow." She didn't turn back, but I knew the tears spilt, because I heard a sob as she closed the door.

After a few moments, my door slammed against the wall as Holland opened it and stared at me for a while before walking in.

"I don't think she betrayed you, honey. You left the door open, so I heard the conversation. Gabe gets too paranoid." She was ready to defend Gabe again, because her eyes looked infuriated.

"Who called my father then?" I asked a little too angrily. The fury hadn't left me.

"Honey, I don't know. They could have planted that here. I mean, they have found us before. Remember the footage from a year ago?" I did. The day was terrible. We watched and waited to be attacked while someone waited just outside the house at the lifeguard chairs. Finally, they left the house untouched, but I knew he worked for my father. "For heaven's sake, we took someone in to test the cure and they exploded right down there. He could have planted false phone calls. I'm confused, but I know she loved you. What if she was working for him and then she stopped because she cared for you?"

I didn't respond, because I didn't believe she loved me at all. "Then she betrayed me," I said finally.

"But love betrayed how she felt before. If she was working with him, he knows where we are. And no one has attacked us yet. Think about that."

I did for a second and I laughed. "He'll be here soon then. I upset her."

Holland smiled. "I don't know what is going on. But I do know that you should go talk to her. You can get past this. Just think about it," she told me.

She got up swiftly and shut the door behind her. I could always count on her to make me feel better. I waited about five minutes and walked to the door. I took a deep breath and decided to talk to Lena. She would be honest if she loved me.

I couldn't help but wonder if she changed her mind about my father. Then why did she and he continue communicating? Or maybe they planted it there so that I would send her away. What if I was giving them what they wanted?

I knocked twice as soon as I reached her room. I walked in slowly and saw she was lying down. One arm hung off the bed and she looked uncomfortable. So I walked to her and lifted her arm slowly. I turned on her lamp beside her bed.

I jumped back and started shouting for help. The next few seconds of my life made me feel as if I had nothing to live for anymore. I began blaring for help. I didn't know what happened next, because Lena was gone. Not dead, but almost. Her eye was completely blackened from the rotting behind them. She was completely rotten and the smell was unbearable. I didn't know what happened, but I did know there was no saving her.

I felt myself losing my grip on the bed, and I fell to the floor. She was sick. There was no denying it, because the rotting remained the same as it once did. I felt the blow to my head, and I was lost to the world.

Chapter Twenty-Four: Nothing Left

I WOKE UP from my trance, and I looked up to the bed where Lena had been, but she was no longer there. Holland stood crying, and Gabe was nowhere in sight. I didn't understand what I was looking at. Lena was dead. She must have been.

"Is she gone?" I asked quietly as I sat up to put my hand to the back of my head. I leaned against the wall and felt hopeless. I didn't want to hear the answer, but I did anyway.

"She's gone. Gabe took her," Holland said between sobs, and I shot up.

"Took her where?" She didn't meet my eyes. I looked around in frantic mode. Where could she be if she wasn't dead? So I asked.

"Is she dead, Holland?" I asked loudly.

"No, Gabe took her to your father," she said in between gasps and sobs.

"Why is she there?" I screamed, and I shot up from the floor fast, ready to attack her. "Was she with him then?" My heart felt as if it were being ripped from my chest.

"Gabe took her so she could live. She didn't want to die. You didn't want her to die either." Holland didn't look to me anymore. She had her face in between her hands.

"What happened? I thought she wasn't sick. Like Gabe said," I shouted.

"We were wrong. She was sick; she was so sick that she reacted to the dye. I want to make a real antidote now. We should have made a real one to begin with." She heaved in between her words. "I feel so bad. This is all our faults. This is all my fault." She sank to the floor and started wailing loudly. I reached to comfort her, but stopped myself because I was sickened at the thought of being near her. Lena didn't deserve this. She never betrayed us. She believed in us to save her, and we let her down. The love of my life was gone forever.

"Holland, I don't understand what just happened." Holland shook her head. "You have taken away the person I love. Even if she was lying, why was I betrayed, too?" I shouted to her. I got up slowly and walked toward her, ready to hurt her. I remembered I was nothing like my father. I clenched my hands.

"Gabe told her you said to leave and this is what you meant. She thought you wanted her to disappear so she did. She was so sick. She just nodded," Holland told me. She forced herself to look at me and didn't cower away. "So this is what you wanted," she screamed back at me.

"Why would he tell her that? Why would you do this to me?" I started to shake furiously all over. Holland shuddered as she cried louder.

"Well, you did tell her to leave when you were yelling at her," she said as tears gushed from her eyes. "We lost her, and the only hope of finding a real cure. She is gone forever."

"Oh. Shut up. You wanted her only for your pathetic tests. I wanted her because she was real. She was mine, and I lost her."

I slouched down and felt empty. Gabe walked in, and I wanted to slap him. "Well, I gave her to your dad.

It was hell. I called him from the number we found in Lena's phone records. He was only about two hours north of us, which on the jetpack takes no time at all. He was helping to cure some kids. But, guys..." He hesitated. "They followed me." I got up and balled my hand, and just as I was about to attach my fist to his face there was rumbling and the floor began to shake underneath my feet. The ceiling began to sprinkle bits of sand down on us. I stood in place, ready to offer myself up so I could be near her once more.

"Who followed you?" Holland shouted above the noise.

"Them." He pointed to the ceiling as a human arm burst through the ceiling.

"What in the hell are they?" Holland screamed as she ran past us.

"They're human robots. Remember your suggestion, Holland," he said sarcastically, but then flailed his arms frantically. "Run, Jared!" Gabe roared to me.

I moved my feet, but I didn't feel as if I was there. I was a pile of Jell-O moving through the room. There were a million arms and legs being pushed through the ceiling, and I was just about to turn to go out of the emergency door when someone landed right in front of me. It was her.

She was beautiful. There was red lipstick on her lips and brown eye shadow along her eyelids. She never wore makeup like this, but she looked extravagant. Her hair was down in soft waves. It was pushed back slightly, revealing that every trace of rotting was gone. She had the cure. Around her neck was her golden necklace that meant so much to her. I wondered why they let her keep that. She wore jeans with a casual gray shirt that grazed her thighs. She looked incredible, and I was in awe at how different she appeared. She was always beautiful, but now she was perfect. I could not find one flaw in her face. She had her chance to kill me, because I would gladly die from her hands, and she knew it. She grabbed my neck with an iron grip and began to choke me. I gasped for air, but immediately calmed down to stare at her. I felt her grip loosen. A sudden realization seemed to hit her, and she dropped me instantly and turned her head to the side in wonder. She reached for my face and conflict covered her eyes.

She knew I was someone she recognized. I saw it in her face, but then her eyes flickered from her normal hazel eyes to a dark emerald. She shook the confusion out of her mind. Her eyes, now the color she feared and had nightmares about, were her own. She smirked at me with taunting eyes. And I screamed as a burning sensation came over my body.

"Help me!" I managed as I fell to the floor in pain. I caught sight of someone running toward Lena with a brick. Holland hit Lena with it before Lena had time to react.She dropped the brick and looked down, conflicted. "Sorry," she said in a melancholy way.

Lena didn't get knocked out, but she did lose her concentration. I ran to the escape door with Holland following me while Lena recovered. I never showed Lena the door out, so she hopefully wouldn't lead anyone to follow us. The door led to a slide into the ocean. Gabe had made it for this exact scenario. We always thought it would be fun to take, but this wasn't fun. Nowhere near fun. We barely made it to the room before I heard the wind blowing strongly outside.

Gabe was already outside by the time I reached the door. It locked down as soon as Holland crossed the doorway. The slide elongated upward from our underground home and into the ocean and was only visible when we hit the button, which Gabe did. We each got onto the slide and a whooshing sound erupted around us as we were suctioned down and landed into the ocean. As I hit the water, I closed my eyes, letting it engulf me. When I opened them I looked above to see at least a thousand figures flying toward us.

"They can fly? Are you joking? I forgot. Damn it!" Holland screamed loudly.

They flew toward us with full speed, but as soon as they approached the ocean, they stopped suddenly, as if something beckoned them to come forward, but they couldn't. All their eyes glowed and they all turned quickly around. They always let us go, and I never knew why. One stayed back, staring and turned away slowly. It was Lena.

"Guys," I said quietly. They both turned to look at me. "I have to go after her. She is still in there. I can try to make her remember me. They wiped her memory. I'm sure of it, but I can bring it back," I told them. "I know I can do it, and she is taken over by these impulses, but what if I can stop them? I have to try or die trying. That is who I love, and I won't live without her." I hesitated and was overwhelmed by how much I would risk saving her. "If she is gone forever, then I will die killing my father and anyone who is with him."

They both looked at me, dazed, but Holland nodded. "Go get her. We'll be there for you. I'm going to stay here and get supplies. There will be war. We have to get her back. She is the key. She is the antidote, Jar."

I smiled and nodded to her; Gabe just nodded swiftly. "I will stay here and work on weapons. Hopefully they won't come back. Try to keep them at bay," he told me. We shook hands, and I held Holland in a hug. We got out of the water after our embrace, and I looked up to the sky. It was clear once more. The water weighed me down and the sand stuck to my body. I needed a change of clothes, but I kept walking. I had plenty of time to get clothes from a store. I walked to the cave where the car was hidden. The Audi that I drove to get Lena here was covered with sand. I looked forward and began driving. I caught sight of Holland and Gabe by the beach, trying to find the way back in. They caught sight of me, and Holland was waving to me and Gabe gave me a thumbs-up and smiled to me.

I drove the car toward the road; toward my love, toward my death. I didn't know which, and I didn't think I cared either way. It led me to her.

Acknowledgements

Thank you to my **mom, dad, Dina, Dimitri, Grandma, Great Grandmother and Susie** for giving me with the courage to write this book. I have many people to thank for the courage I have now.

I want to thank **Edee** for being there for me when I was still learning the ropes of book writing. I will always remember you and what you have done for me.

Thank you, **Ron,** for taking my pictures. They are amazing and I can't thank you enough.

Thank you to my editor, **Measha,** for being awesome and my second pair of eyes. You let me know what worked and what didn't. You have changed the story in the best way possible.

Thank you to **Ashley** for listening to my vision. I could never have had my dream cover without you.

Thank you to my family for listening to me ramble on to you about wanting to write this book. All of you have believed in me and I'm blessed to have the biggest support system.

To my **mom**, who always told me to never give up even when I felt like I was going fail. You always told me I would make it happen if I put faith in myself first.

To my **dad**, who encouraged me and always believed in me, even when I was unsure.

To **Dimitri**, who always told me I could make it and that I was crazy not to try. And for always telling me that I will make it "big time."

To **Dina**, who listened to me and encouraged me to do this. We both are going to do great things one day.

Finally, **thank you** for reading my first book.

About the Author

Taylor Hondos attends the University of North Carolina at Greensboro, studying English Literature. In high school she began writing "Antidote" and finished writing it by the end of her freshman year of college. "Antidote" is the first book in the Antidote trilogy. She plans to release "Prospect" next year. She lives with her family in North Carolina.

More Books from Patchwork Press

Mortality by Kellie Sheridan After surviving a deadly plague outbreak, sixteen-year-old Savannah thought she had lived through the very worst of human history. There was no way to know that the miracle vaccine would put everyone at risk for a fate worse than un-death. Now, two very different kinds of infected walk the Earth, intent on nothing but feeding and destroying what little remains of civilization. When the inoculated are bitten, infection means watching on in silent horror as self-control disappears and the idea of feasting on loved ones becomes increasingly hard to ignore. Starving and forced to live inside of the abandoned high school, all Savannah wants is the chance to fight back. When a strange boy arrives with a plan to set everything right, she gets her chance. Meeting Cole changes everything. Mere survival will never be enough.

Ignite by Erica Crouch
Penemuel (Pen) fell from grace over a millennium ago, yet there are still times she questions her decision to follow her twin brother, Azael, to Hell. Now that the archangel Michael has returned, threatening Lucifer's vie for the throne, she begins questioning everything she has always believed.

As Hell prepares for war - spreading a demonic virus and pilfering innocent souls to build an army - the lines separating the worlds blur. Fates erase and the future is left unwritten. Azael is determined that he and his sister will continue to serve as demons together, but for the first time in her life, Pen is not ruled by destiny. She has the freedom of choice.

With choice comes sacrifice, and Pen must decide which side she's willing to risk everything fighting for: the light, or the dark.

Frost by E. Latimer Megan Walker's touch has turned to ice. She can't stop the frost, and the consequences of her first kiss are horrifying.

When her new powers attract attention, Megan finds herself caught up in an ancient war between Norse giants. One side fuelled by a mad queen's obsession and an ancient prophecy about Ragnarök, the other by an age-old grudge. Both sides believe Megan to be something she's not. Both sides will stop at nothing to have her.

Fire or frost. It's an impossible decision, but she'll have to act soon, because the storm is coming.

Taylor Hondos